Chicago's Sweetest '16:

A Baseball Fantasy

By Steve Corman

Steve Corman Books

Chicago's Sweetest '16: A Baseball Fantasy

Published in the United States of America

Actual players and personnel of both the Cubs and White Sox teams for 2016 were employees of the organizations on November 1, 2015. Players and personnel of the teams during the 1906 World Series and the histories of the teams were real people. All others are fictional characters not based on any single person.

ISBN: 978-0-692-55072-4

Dedicated to the outstanding baseball
minds and great personalities of two
long-time colleagues and dear friends:

John Wallenstein
A Staunch Lifelong White Sox Fan

Bill Gutman
A Cubs Supporter Forever

Both may have departed, but are still
watching, relishing and cheering at a
feverish pitch for their teams during
every second of this memorable White
Sox and Cubs Crosstown World Series.

CHAPTERS

PREFACE

I'll never forget the day I attended my first major league baseball game when I was just 9 years old in 1951.

The Chicago White Sox were playing the old St. Louis Browns two years before they moved to Baltimore. On that day, ageless Satchel Paige was one of the pitchers the Browns brought out of the bullpen at Comiskey Park.

I was awestruck as I saw his famed windmill windup and amazed when my father told me how old he might be. With Satchel, you never knew for certain.

A few weeks later, I saw my first National League game at Wrigley Field when the New York Giants visited the Chicago Cubs. Many people around us were abuzz over the Giants new, very young center fielder Willie Mays, who was being described as a future superstar.

Seeing Willie and Satchel at the beginning and end of their brilliant careers made me an instant fan for life.

I began asking an endless number of questions about what to me will always be America's pastime and number one sport. Questions such as when did the White Sox and Cubs last play against one another in a World Series?

When I learned it was 1906, my response was, "Wow, that was 45 years ago! How could they go so long without playing for the championship?"

Little did I know then that it would grow to be 110 years. But now, times have finally changed and the promise of this dream is about to become realized in 2016.

This, of course, comes after the Cubs incredible 2015 performance in which they won 97 games during the regular season. They proceeded to flourish in the playoffs, winning a play-in game over the Pittsburgh Pirates, eliminating the St. Louis Cardinals in the first round before being swept by the New York Mets for the National League pennant.

Sit back and enjoy the dream come true for millions of baseball fans around the world, along with a look back in time to 1906.

Steve Corman

Chapter 1 – A Dream Come True

Sitting majestically on the shores of Lake Michigan, there's no doubt Chicago is a world class city. Its stunning architecture captivates millions of visitors and residents each and every day. Legendary writer and poet Carl Sandburg referred to Chicago as standing tall with massive broad shoulders.

The city's beautiful landscape is enticing, endearing and romantic. A wide array of cultural gems such as the Art Institute, Museum of Science and Industry, Field Museum, Shedd Aquarium and Adler Planetarium (just to name a few) shine with aesthetic magnificence. There's also a first-rate symphony, opera company and ballet troupe.

The weather and baseball teams though? That's entirely another story.

But on this late October day, SURPRISE: Light snow is falling this morning with tonight marking the start of the World Series.

This 2016 edition isn't like any ordinary fall classic. This time the participants are two teams who until last year have seldom achieved lofty heights: the Chicago White Sox and Chicago Cubs. In fact, they've only met in the World Series once before. That was years ago in 1906. The Cubs were considered baseball's crème de la crème and romped to the National League pennant with 116 wins and only 36 losses, 20 games ahead of the New York Giants. The winning percentage of .763 remains the best all-time in Major League Baseball history. (1) The 2001 Seattle Mariners also won 116 games but lost 46, so their winning percentage was .716. (2)

The White Sox also had a solid record with 93 victories. They were often referred to as "the hitless wonders," with a combined team batting average of just .230 and a total of 7 home runs for the entire season. (3)

Now, more than a century later, this time in late October, with the same two teams ready to meet in the World Series, and very coincidentally, it's snowing lightly, just like in 1906. Whoever heard of October snow in Chicago?

World Series games now are always played at night, as opposed to exclusively during daylight. This time around, the World Series starts later in the month since there were several rounds of elimination playoffs among the five teams from each league who advance.

The first two games are being played at what is now known as U.S. Cellular Field, opened in 1991 to replace the original Comiskey Park across the street. The old park was built and opened in 1910 on the city's south side at 35th Street and Shields. The team's owner Charles Comiskey built that 45,000 seat ballpark as a tribute to himself.

Chicago is bubbling over and beaming with pride over this surprising World Series match-up. The Cubs had a standout season in 2015 as their young players jelled into an exciting, winning ball club, under new manager Joe Maddon and advanced to baseball's playoff round.

They won the first-round play-in game against the Pittsburgh Pirates 4-0 behind the great effort by pitching standout Jake Arrieta and home runs from Kyle Schwarber and Dexter Fowler and then battled their way through the next round to defeat the always tough St. Louis Cardinals.

Now it's a year later and the Cubs are back again, bigger and stronger, meeting a White Sox team that barely made its way into the playoffs.

The White Sox, inconsistent and very mediocre at times in 2015, greatly improved in 2016, surprising everyone by just squeezing their way into the playoffs.

Fans were beginning to arrive by mid-afternoon, bundled up on this chilly to cold October day, anxiously awaiting the 7pm start. Once the gates opened at 5pm, there were nearly 20,000 people milling about.

"Hello, what a great, great day and night this is," the middle-aged man says to the young couple sitting next to him along the third base side, about 20 rows back. "It's a dream come true for every baseball fan here in Chicago."

"I'm Jeff O'Fallon. My great-great-great grandfather was a sportswriter with the old *Chicago Gazette* and he covered the 1906 White Sox-Cubs World Series. I'm also a free-lance writer for several magazines."

"That's incredible," replies the young woman, sporting a bright, blue Chicago Cubs 2015 playoffs sweatshirt over her very pregnant belly. "I'm Katie Sorensen and this is my husband Tom Buchanan. He's a Sox fan as you can probably tell from his shirt."

It's quite apparent from the start that she has a bubbly, exuberant personality and is a perfect match for her husband. He's a bit more withdrawn and intense but obviously is very proud of her and very much in love with this striking red-headed woman with freckles scattered around her smiling face.

 She's only about 5 feet, 4 inches tall but seems taller with her energy and strong character, a big reason for her success as an accountant. She's very bright and astute, and her mind seems to work a mile a minute.

Tom is about 5 feet 10 inches with dark hair and a strong presence. He's an attorney with a large Chicago law firm that specializes in employment discrimination cases.

 "I guess your allegiance to different Chicago teams hasn't affected your marriage. Congratulations on the impending arrival," O'Fallon says. "Do you know if it's a boy or a girl?"

 "No, we want to be surprised, but we do have names picked out. And each one combines a White Sox and Cub player. If it's a girl, she'll be Gabrielle (after Gabby Hartnett, the great Cub catcher), Minnie (after Orestes "Minnie" Minoso, the White Sox longtime, standout outfielder who should be in the Hall of Fame).

And if it's a boy, he'll be Frank (after Frank Thomas, the White Sox Hall of Famer), Ernie (after Ernie Banks, the Cubs Hall of Famer)," Buchanan explains. "Right now we're just hoping Katie can hold off having this child until after the World Series."

"Did you two meet by any chance at a baseball game?" Jeff further asks.

"Yes, definitely yes," Katie blurts out. "But it wasn't with just one of our Chicago teams. It was the White Sox and Cubs exhibition game in 1994 at Wrigley Field. That was the last time they played for charity before inter-league play started the next year."

"And didn't you also see an extraordinary basketball player in that game?" Jeff adds.

"Of course, Michael Jordan played right field for the Sox and hit a double down the left field line," Tom replies. "We've gone to just about every Sox-Cubs inter-league game, the two games in Chicago when the White Sox swept Houston to win the 2005 World Series and, of course, last year's Cubs playoff games against the Cardinals and Mets that were played here at Wrigley Field."

"I was so thrilled about last year's incredible young team and now this is the ultimate with the Sox and

Cubs meeting for the championship," Katie adds. "We were in junior high school when we met, got married in our mid 20s and are just starting a family now in our 30s. In fact, after the Cubs lost to the Mets for the pennant, we vowed to work very hard to get me pregnant and now look at me. I'm due just about the time when the Cubs will be winning the World Series."

"That's all great. It's nice to show such incredible passion for your two hometown teams and now share it with your soon to be born child," Jeff interjects.

"So, have you heard stories about the 1906 World Series from your father and grandfather?" Tom asks him.

"Absolutely! We've always been a big baseball family, both playing the game and following the teams. My grandfather on my mother's side, Sid Schweger, was an All-American catcher at the University of Illinois but never played professionally. He became an accountant so he could have a steady income. It was much different then."

"I've heard the entire story of the 1906 Series endless times and am happy to share it with you while we're here tonight and I assume you might be at more than just game one," the writer adds.

"Yes, it cost us a fortune, but we were able to get tickets for each game, not necessarily in this location, but we can meet you before the games for a bite to eat," Katie replies. "I can't believe how fortunate we are to have met you here. So are all your family members native Chicago people?"

"Most certainly, my great-great-great grandfather, Patrick O'Shea, was born during the Great Chicago Fire in 1871. They lived on DeKoven Street, about five blocks west of where Mrs. O'Leary's cow supposedly kicked over the lantern that set almost the whole town ablaze and destroyed virtually everything in its path." Jeff explains.

"The Great Chicago Fire was a monster that burned from Sunday, October 8th to early Tuesday, October 10, 1871. The fire killed almost 300 people, destroyed roughly 3 and a half square miles of Chicago and left more than 100,000 residents homeless, including my family and relatives."

"He was born at the old Mercy Hospital on October 9th. His parents, like many others, fled to Mercy Hospital, which was then located at Rush Street and the Chicago River, for safety. That site was later the Chicago Sun-Times and Daily News building, and now is the Trump Tower."

"Oh, Gosh!" Katie excitedly chimes in. "That's where I'm having my baby. Of course, it's now located very close to this ballpark, around 23rd and South Michigan."

The countdown continues to the start of the 2016 World Series. It's starting at U.S. Cellular Field because the American League won July's All-Star Game. That became the determining factor under the regime of former baseball commissioner Bud Selig, instead of alternating each year which league had home field advantage.

That's the way it had been, with few exceptions, since 1924. The 1945 series, between the Cubs and Tigers, was changed because of the war.

There was strong speculation that Selig's replacement, Rob Manfred, would reverse that decision, but nothing has happened yet.

"Did you know that prior to 1924, the pattern had been to alternate by game or to make another arrangement convenient for both clubs?" Jeff asks them. "The participating teams could determine the order in which city the games would be played. In the 1906 series, as an example, games alternated between Cubs and White Sox home fields since they were just a few miles apart and a flip of a coin determined who would go first."

"While we're waiting for the game to begin, let me tell you about the 1906 series and some of the incredible players in those games. Their stories are so different than what we hear about modern era athletes. I learned about them from my Dad and Granddad who were told the tales from my great-great-great-grandfather and his son."

Chapter 2 – Game 1 – October 9, 1906
World Series
"The Barker's Call"

Game one of the 1906 World Series took place on a cool, early October day amid snow flurries at West Side Park. That was the Cubs home field at 912 South Wood Street, where the University of Illinois Medical Center is now located.

The Cubs played there from 1893 until 1915 and won over 1,000 games during that time as well as the 1907 and 1908 World Series. There's a plaque at that location sponsored by the Way Out in Left Field Society, the Illinois Medical District, the State Historical Society and the University of Illinois at Chicago. It was placed there in 2008. (4)

On this day, a crowd of 12,693 people were on hand at the ballpark, about half the capacity because of the weather, and others listened to the call of the game at two different locations. (5)

"Ladies and gentlemen, here are the starting lineups for both the White Sox and Cubs…" a barker holding a large megaphone blurted out.

Since there were no radio stations until 1920 and few people had access to teletype machines or sports tickers, keeping track of the flow of each game was very challenging and difficult.

In that era, a great deal of news we customarily now learn about within hours, even minutes, after an event or tragedy happens, didn't become common knowledge for a day or two. The biggest story of the year was the devastating San Francisco earthquake on Wednesday, April 18th in which more 500 people were killed and 80% of the city was destroyed by three days of fires. Even then President Theodore Roosevelt didn't learn about it right away. Neither did the majority of the 85 million residents in the United States.

The *Chicago Tribune* newspaper set up listening sites in the Auditorium Theatre on Congress Street at Wabash Avenue. Designed by renowned architects Louis Sullivan and Dankmar Adler, it's still an active venue seating 4,000.

Considered one of the most acoustically perfect gathering spots in the world, many of the most renowned singers and musicians have performed there. They range from Frank Sinatra to Itzhak

Perlman to Smokey Robinson. Speakers have included both Presidents Roosevelt and William McKinley, along with others like Booker T. Washington. More recently the Auditorium was the site of the 2015 National Football League player draft and was there again this past spring.

The other listening location was the First Regiment Armory at 16th Street and South Michigan Avenue, which held 5,000 and was demolished in 1968.

Each stage had a 20-foot tall baseball diamond. Balls and strikes were indicated by light bulbs in the early days of electricity. Batter's names were also illuminated. Lightbulbs attached to the bases were turned on to indicate base runners. The announcer described the play as it came over the ticker. That's the same premise later used to recreate baseball games via radio broadcasts.

"Picture yourself at this memorable ballpark for Game 1 with snowflakes falling," Jeff suggests.

"Today's starting pitchers – for the Cubs Mordecai "Three Finger" Brown and for the White Sox Nick Altrock," the barker alerted the audience at one of the downtown sites.

Most baseball writers and analysts predicted the great-hitting Cubs team would easily win this edition of the World Series.

One exception was the *Tribune's* Hugh Fullerton, who picked the White Sox to win the series in six games. That information was never seen in print during the series. His editor was afraid of the public's angry reaction and didn't publish his theory until the series was over. The main reason for this bold prediction was the White Sox American League record of 19 consecutive wins in a row over the month of August. During that time, the so-called "hitless wonders" outscored their opponents 100 to 24. (6)

Opening ceremonies featured the presentation of "loving cups" to both teams, followed by the bundled-up fans at the ballpark singing "Auld Lang Syne."

"First batter for the White Sox, right fielder Ed "Cookie" Hahn," the field announcer yelled out loudly to the crowd through his megaphone.

Hahn stepped in and the 1906 World Series was underway.

Cubs starting pitcher Brown was the ace of the pitching staff. He won 20 games that year with a remarkable 1.04 earned run average (ERA), third lowest in the history of the game. (7)

Born into a farming family in Nyesville, Indiana, Brown's nickname was the result of his pitching hand being maimed by a corn shredder as a youngster. He lost one finger and had two others seriously damaged. But as a teenager he discovered the deformed hand enabled him to throw a wicked curve ball which fooled hitters for many years.

Overall in his career, Brown won 239 games and had a career ERA of 2.06. He was eventually elected to baseball's Hall of Fame. (8)

For the White Sox, the starting pitcher in this World Series opener normally would have been fast-balling ace right-hander "Big Ed" Walsh, another future Hall of Famer.

His best pitch was a devastating spitball, which was legal at that time, but his saliva froze on the baseball in the chilly conditions and limited its effectiveness. Player-manager Fielder Jones instead opted for another right-hander, Altrock.

Both pitchers were perfect through three innings. The White Sox finally broke the ice in the top of the fifth. George Rohe hit a triple down the left-field line and scored on an error. They added another run in the sixth on singles by Jones and Frank Isbell.

The Cubs quickly put runners at second and third with no one out in the bottom of the sixth and it became a one-run game when Altrock threw a wild pitch. However, they couldn't get the tying run home.

After the final out in the ninth for a 2-1 White Sox victory, many of their fans ran exuberantly onto the field to celebrate.

Player-manager Jones, the center fielder, did a joyous dance before he caught the long fly ball to end it.

Afterwards, he told members of the press, "It's great to get off on such a high note without even using our ace pitcher. Nick was great today and really shut them down after they got those runners on base in the sixth. I can't wait for tomorrow's game back on our home field."

Cubs owner Charles Murphy, who had purchased the team in 1905 for the then hefty sum of $125,000, took it all in stride, smugly saying, "One swallow does not make a summer." (9)

Rohe, who hit the triple and scored the winning run, was a utility infielder. He was with the New Orleans

Pelicans in 1904 and was the team captain of the pennant winning team before a yellow fever epidemic broke up the league.

"Comiskey purchased his contract in 1905 and he spent most of his time with the Sox sitting on the bench. The only reason he was playing in the World Series was that regular second baseman George Davis sustained an injury and couldn't play. It may have been the best thing to happen to the Sox," O'Fallon continues.

"It turned out the he and Jiggs Donahue tied for the highest batting average in the series at .333. Many said it was divine intervention that Davis was injured and Rohe replaced him in the line-up. By the way, Rohe hit a bases loaded triple in game 3 to help the Sox win that game also. After the Series was over, Comiskey made a promise, somewhat foolishly, to the fans, 'Whatever George Rohe may do from now on, he's signed for life with me!'

"Not surprisingly, Rohe was released after the 1907 season and never played another game in the major leagues. Perhaps more notably, he is credited with having "Shoeless" Joe Jackson sign a major league contract with the Cleveland Indians. That was before he was traded to the South Side team. In his later years, Rohe changed his career and became a commercial photographer. (10)

"Johnny Kling was the starting Cubs catcher. His family expected him to go to work in the bakery business, but he loved baseball and was able to make a career out of playing it. Even more than baseball, he loved shooting pool and played competitively to help him make a living.

"He began his baseball career with the Chicago Orphans, who as we know were re-named the Cubs. He was a great defensive catcher which would come to light in the 1906 World Series. He also held the record in Major League Baseball with 12 hits in a row in 1902. It was tied by Walt Dropo in 1952, but not surpassed until 1979! He was also unusual, because he did not smoke, drink or chew tobacco.

"In 1906, he announced he wanted a new contract with a raise. If he didn't get it he'd stay home and play pool. Luckily for the Cubs, he changed his mind and played. In the off season between 1906 and 1910, he won both the World Billiards and World's Pool championships. Baseball writers have called him one

of the greatest catchers in Chicago Cubs history,"
O'Fallon concludes. (11)

It was now almost time, in the current year of 2016,
for pre-game festivities to start, including player
interviews.

"Let's meet before tomorrow's game in the White
Sox Bards Room for an early dinner on me," O'Fallon
tells his new-found friends Katie Sorensen and Tom
Buchanan. "I'll give you a rundown on game two from
1906 and tell you some more stories about different
players from that era. Enjoy tonight's game. I know I
will."

Chapter 3 – Over the Years

While they're often referred to as Chicago's "lovable losers," the Cubs actually have a better record and have appeared in more World Series games than the White Sox. Of course, they've been around 30 years longer.

The Cubs started in 1871 as the White Stockings in an independent league and joined the National League when it began in 1876. They changed their name 19 years later in 1890 to the Colts, then again in 1898 to the Orphans before permanently becoming the Chicago Cubs in 1903. (12)

With all those different names, the franchise has won 10,611 games, including both regular and post season contests. They also have an overall record above .500 with 10,134 losses, both numbers coming through the 2015 season.

The White Sox, on the other hand, began as a franchise in 1901 with the start of the American League and also have an overall record above .500 for both regular and post season play. They've won 9,004 and lost 8,847. (13)

Both teams have had many good moments, along with some terrible times.

For example, White Sox teams between 1951 and 1967 had 17 consecutive finishes above .500, winning 90 or more games seven different times. Yet they only won the pennant once during that run. That was in 1959 when they lost the World Series in six games to the Los Angeles Dodgers, who bounced back gallantly after being steamrolled 11-0 in the opening game.

The Cubs had two long runs of winning seasons. They put together 14 consecutive above .500 campaigns between 1926 and 1939, and also managed to string 12 years in a row above .500 between 1903 and 1914.

The North Side team also has had five seasons with 100 or more wins (1906, 1907, 1909, 1910 and 1935) while the White Sox only won 100 games once during a single year!

In terms of the World Series for the ultimate prize, the White Sox have won three of them. They came in 1906 against the Cubs, in 1917 when they beat the New York Giants and again in 2005 in a sweep over the Houston Astros.

The Cubs have won just two, both against superstar Ty Cobb and the Detroit Tigers in 1907 and 1908,
the years following the only all-Chicago
championship.

But the Cubs have been in a total of 10 World
Series, losing 8 of them. Their last appearance was
71 years ago in 1945 when they were beaten 4
games to 3 by Detroit.

There have been less than memorable World Series
escapades for both Chicago teams. First and most
well-known was the infamous Black Sox scandal
involving the alleged fixing of games by the White Sox
in the 1919 series against the Cincinnati Reds.

Team owner Charles Comiskey was disliked by
many of his players, primarily for being a cheapskate.
He long had a reputation for underpaying his players
and reneging on promises of salary increases and
bonuses. This happened even though they were one
of the league's best teams and had won the 1917
World Series.

Before the 1919 series began, there were wide-
spread rumors that it was being fixed by disgruntled
White Sox players who had allegedly been
approached by gamblers. The clubhouse was

reportedly divided into two factions, clean players who wanted nothing to do with giving away games and dirty players who intentionally played poorly to ensure White Sox defeats to get even with Comiskey.

When all was said and done, Cincinnati won the unusually long nine-game series, 5 games to 3. Gamblers had started betting heavily on the Reds at the same time the rumors of a fix came to light.

It took nearly a year before a grand jury was convened in 1920 to pursue the issue. Eight White Sox players and five gamblers were charged with conspiracy to defraud and faced trial. Even though they were unanimously acquitted, baseball commissioner Kennesaw "Mountain" Landis suspended the eight players from ever playing professional baseball again.

Included among the group was the best White Sox player, center fielder "Shoeless" Joe Jackson. Baseball writers and analysts feel Jackson's entry into the Hall of Fame would have been a certainty if not for his suspension. Newer research shows he never accepted any money and presumably was not involved in the fix.

Landis later explained his decision, "Regardless of the verdict of juries, no player who throws a ball game, no player who undertakes or promises to throw a ball game, no player who sits in confidence with a bunch of crooked ballplayers and gamblers, where the ways and means of throwing a game are discussed and does not promptly tell his club about it, will ever play professional baseball." (14)

The Cubs were also involved in a bizarre situation in the 1932 World Series against the New York Yankees, nothing as severe as allegedly fixing games, but a significant event nevertheless.

It involved legendary slugger Babe Ruth in game three at Wrigley Field in Chicago. Before the start of the game, the tension between the teams was high. "Trash-talking" of the day was at its peak between the two teams. Both the Cubs players and their fans were particularly focused on shouting out vile taunts toward the Babe. .

The score was tied 4-4 in the 5th inning when Ruth came to the plate against pitcher Charlie Root. With the count 2-2, Babe stepped back out of the batter's box for a moment and apparently gestured toward center field. He then proceeded to smash a long, booming home run over the wall near the flagpole in center field. Some say it was the longest home run up to that time at Wrigley Field.

When he crossed home plate, Ruth could no longer hide his smile as he was patted by his exuberant teammates when he reached the Yankees dugout.

Shortly after the apparent "called shot", the Chicago-based Curtiss Candy Company, makers of the popular Baby Ruth candy bar, installed a large advertising sign on the rooftop of one of the apartment buildings on Sheffield Avenue. The sign, reading "Baby Ruth", was just across the street from where Ruth's home run had landed.

Until the 1970s, when the aging sign was taken down, Cubs fans at Wrigley Field had to endure this not-so-subtle reminder of the "called shot."

Root was left in the game, but for only one pitch, which Lou Gehrig drilled into the right field seats for his second homer of the day. The Yankees won the game 7–5, and the next day they finished off the demoralized Cubs 13–6, completing the four-game sweep.

Among many dignitaries attending the game was then New York Governor Franklin Delano Roosevelt, soon to be elected the 32nd President of the United States. FDR reportedly had a laugh as he watched Ruth round the bases.

The debate has lingered for decades over whether Ruth actually pointed to center field, as many claim, or was just waving the bat in the direction of the pitcher.

The Cubs enjoyed one more pennant at the close of World War II finishing 98–56. Due to wartime travel restrictions, the first three games of the 1945 World Series were played in Detroit, where the Cubs won two games, including a one-hitter by pitcher Claude Passeau, and the final four were played at Wrigley. (15)

In Game 4 of the Series, the Curse of the Billy Goat was allegedly laid upon the Cubs when owner P.K. Wrigley ejected Chicago restaurant entrepreneur Billy Sianis, who had come to Game 4 with two box seat tickets, one for him and one for his goat. They paraded around for a few innings, but Wrigley demanded the goat leave the park due to its unpleasant odor. Upon his ejection, Mr. Sianis supposedly uttered, *"The Cubs, they ain't gonna win no more."* (16)

The Cubs lost Game 4, as well as the Series, and have not been back since. Many believe Sianis put a "curse" on the Cubs, apparently preventing the team from playing in the World Series. After losing the 1945 World Series to the Tigers, the Cubs finished with winning seasons the next two years, but neither team made it to post-season play.

The Cubs played mostly forgettable baseball, finishing among the worst teams in the National League on an almost annual basis for many years to come between the 1950s and with a few exceptions, until the early 1990s. Longtime infielder/manager Phil Cavarretta, who had been a key player in the '45 season, was fired during spring training in 1954 after admitting the team was unlikely to finish above fifth place.

The team's second baseman between 1948 and 1950 was journeyman Emil Verban, best known for his solid defense on the field. He had previously played for the Cardinals and Phillies, and hit a solid .412 (7 for 12) in the 1944 all-St. Louis World Series in which the Cardinals beat the Browns.

As a tribute to him, a group of die-hard Cubs fans based in Washington, DC, formed the Emil Verban

Society in 1975. Its purpose was to honor him as a Cub player who epitomizes being competent on the baseball diamond although obscure, while believing in a strong work ethic and playing hard every day.

To become a member of the Verban Society, which includes 2016 Democratic Presidential Candidate Hillary Clinton and former Republican Vice-President Dick Cheney, you have to be a life-long, long-suffering, die-hard follower of the Cubs and be willing to accept misfortune and misery as a baseball fan.

Years later he was invited to Washington to meet then President Ronald Reagan, also a Society member, at the White House. Verban died in 1989 at the age of 73. (17)

Hall of Fame shortstop Ernie Banks, later known as Mr. Cub, would become one of the star players in the league for many years, beginning in 1954. While he was a standout at shortstop and later first base, finding help for him proved a difficult task. Quality players like sluggers Hank Sauer and Ralph Kiner were few and far between.

Combine that with poor ownership decisions such as the College of Coaches, who each rotated as team manager during the season, and the ill-fated trade of future Hall of Famer Lou Brock to the Cardinals for pitcher Ernie Broglio (who won only 7 games over the next three seasons), greatly hampered on-field performance.

After owning the franchise for 60 years, the team was surprisingly sold by the Wrigley family to the Chicago Tribune Company in 1981 for $20.5 million.

On July 6, 2009, wealthy business executive Tom Ricketts and family reached an agreement with the Tribune Company to purchase the Cubs, Wrigley Field, and 25% of Comcast SportsNet Chicago for close to $900 million. The contract was sent to then commissioner Bud Selig for approval.

Three months later the other MLB owners approved the sale by a unanimous vote. On October 27, 2009, the Ricketts family officially took over 95% ownership of the Chicago Cubs and Wrigley Field and 25% ownership of Comcast SportsNet Chicago. The Tribune retained 5% ownership of the team. (18)

One of Ricketts' first announced plans was a massive renovation and rebuilding of Wrigley Field, which opened nearly a century earlier in 1916 as Weeghman Park after the name of the then-owner of the team.

It took almost two years for the new ownership to start making significant front-office moves, but they were successful in getting the man they wanted to become President of Baseball Operations.

Theo Epstein took over that job in October, 2011 and had big goals from the start but cautioned it would take time and involve a major rebuilding of all aspects of the organization.

He was the youngest General Manager in baseball history to lead a team to a World Series title when the Red Sox won the championship in 2004, two years after he was named to that position. It was the team's first title in 86 years and he repeated the achievement three years later in 2007. That's exactly what he hoped to accomplish with the Cubs and the winning began in earnest in 2015.

Just like he did with the Red Sox, Epstein wasted little time changing the entire look of the team on the field, focusing on developing promising young players with a huge upside.

One of his first moves was to dismiss manager Mike Quade, who had earned good marks while moving up through the ranks. There were some signs of encouragement during the 2011 season, yet the team still finished with 91 losses and 20 games under the .500 mark.

Next in line to lead the team on the field was Dale Sveum, from Pinole, California, in the San Francisco Bay Area. He was a career major league shortstop and solid utility player, spending 12 years in the big show between 1986 and 1999 with seven different teams, mostly the Milwaukee Brewers.

Sveum's overall batting average was .236. He hit a total of 69 home runs, with 25 of them coming during his second season in 1987.

As the Cubs manager in 2012 and 2013, Sveum was mediocre at best, losing 197 games during his years in the hot seat. He worked well, baseball people said, with the team's steady parade of young hopefuls, helping them become true major league prospects.

Sveum did, by the way, come out smelling like a rose. He was hired by the Kansas City Royals as hitting coach and the team proceeded to win the American League pennant and come within one out of taking the World Series in 2014.

Former San Diego Padres bench coach Rick Renteria was next to take on the role of manager. His

2014 team showed some encouraging signs, posting a record of 73 wins and 89 losses, and it was announced that he would return for another year.

Not too long after the 2014 season ended, a loophole in the contract of highly regarded Tampa Bay manager Joe Maddon, suddenly made him available to be hired by another team, most likely the highest bidder. The Cubs didn't waste any time and signed him to a robust five-year contract. Maddon became the team's 54th manager in its long history.

So, after telling Renteria he'd been rehired, Epstein instead found himself in the embarrassing situation of having to dismiss him. The Cubs issued a lengthy statement explaining the circumstances with Epstein praising his former team leader.

"Rick's sterling reputation should only be enhanced by his season as Cubs manager. We challenged Rick to create an environment in which our young players could develop and thrive at the big league level and he succeeded. Working with the youngest team in the league and an imperfect roster, he had the club playing hard and improving throughout the season. His passion, character, optimism and work ethic showed up every day," he said. (19)

Epstein and general manager Jed Hoyer were just getting started, along with Maddon. They successfully concluded their much-publicized attempt to sign prize left-handed pitcher Jon Lester by agreeing with him on a six-year, $155 million deal. The former Boston Red Sox and Oakland A's star was thrilled about his new baseball home. (20)

So was Maddon. "This definitely propels us into Plan A, which is kind of neat. It's a big day for us moving forward," he said in the lobby of the Manchester Grand Hyatt in San Diego after the deal was announced. "It's not often you get to win the lottery. We won the baseball lottery so far this year. It's up to us now to put it in effect. It's all theory right now. We've got to make it real. But you need pieces like this to make it real." (21)

Chapter 4: The Elusive Playoffs

So, just how did the White Sox and Cubs both manage what seemed like the impossible and earn their way into the 2016 World Series?

For so many years, if one team was good, the other was somewhere between average, mediocre or just plain putrid.

Besides the 1906 World Series, the only other time in their history that both teams moved into the playoffs was in 2008. The White Sox ended the season in an American League Central division tie with Minnesota, but beat the Twins 1-0 in a playoff on a home run by slugger Jim Thome and shutout pitching by John Danks. That gave them an 89-74 record, but they lost in the first round of the playoffs 3 games to 1 to the Tampa Bay Rays, who were then managed by Maddon.

The Cubs fared better, capturing the National League Central with 97 victories. They also were quickly swept away in three games by the Los Angeles Dodgers.

That was the last year either team made it to post-season play until the Cubs remarkable 2015 season. Prior to that, the Cubs finished fifth in the NL Central five consecutive years between 2010 and 2014, going through three different managers in that span. During three of those seasons, they consecutively lost 91,101 and 96 games.

The Cubs in 2015

In the Cubs world, however, shortstop Starlin Castro and first baseman Anthony Rizzo continued to greatly improve over the past two years. There were also several newcomers including second baseman Javier Baez, third baseman Kris Bryant, outfielders Jorge Soler and Chris Coghlan as well as promising pitchers Jake Arrieta, Kyle Hendricks and Jason Hammel, among many others.

Their season began with the Wrigley Field renovation work. It was expected to cost $575 million and take up to four years to complete. Opening night, a nationally televised Easter Sunday match-up against the much-despised St. Louis Cardinals, was played amid bizarre conditions. The onslaught of extremely bad winter weather, with frequent bitter cold and snowy days and weeks, greatly slowed the first phase of construction. That included the demolition and rebuilding of the famed left and right field bleachers, which were not finished and wouldn't be until May or June.

"It looks like Baghdad," Hammel told the *Chicago Business Journal.* "But you know there's a pot of gold at the end of the rainbow. We're going to deal with it, because it's exciting." (22)

It wasn't too exciting in terms of the score for Jon Lester's debut in a Cubs uniform. They lost 3-0 to the Cardinals and their ace pitcher Adam Wainwright. Lester gave up all three runs in just under five innings, but showed solid presence on the mound.

"The ballpark was absolutely electric," Maddon was quick to tell the *Chicago Tribune* after the game. "Pregame was wonderful. Everything was great. We just have to come through with a couple knocks now and then, but we will. I thought it was a really, really - for lack of a better term - a really good night." (23)

Unfortunately, it wasn't such a good night for many of the 35,055 fans who braved the chilly temperature. The team neglected to bring in additional restrooms to compensate for those closed off due to construction.

As a result, hundreds, perhaps even thousands, of fans were lined up to use the existing facilities. The average wait was about two full innings until they could get into a bathroom and finally get back to their seats.

Many men were so frustrated and impatient that they slinked off to a corner location and opted to use their beer cups as pee spittoons.

Cubs management profusely apologized the next day and assured everyone there would be plenty of facilities, albeit portable ones, available for future games.

The Cubs, meantime, started playing extremely well toward the end of April. With Rizzo and Starlin beginning to hit like they previously had, and Bryant making his presence being felt after a brief stint at Triple A Iowa, the team rose to a 12-7 record. By May 11th, they were 15-15 but clearly felt the best was yet to come.

"We're a lot better than a .500 team," pitcher Hendricks told the *Chicago Tribune* after Milwaukee catcher Martin Maldonado hit a bases-loaded single with one out in the 11th inning off Jason Motte to hand the Cubs a 3-2 loss. "We've been losing some games we should have won. We know we can beat these teams and know we will once we get rolling." (24)

And he was right! The Cubs put together a six-game winning streak, four of them over the New York Mets. Included among those victories was Maddon's 800th as a major league manager.

Later in May, the Cubs won a game over Washington 3-2 that featured a monster home run by Bryant off the new left field electronic video board. It was measured at 477 feet, a clout that had rarely, if ever been seen before in Wrigleyville.

Maddon had nothing but compliments for his future superstar and told the *Chicago Tribune* he takes it all in stride, "I think it's up to the guy receiving all the attention to set the tone for everybody else and I think he does. He's very likeable, he's very professional. He doesn't draw it to himself. It just comes to him. I think he's done everything absolutely the right way." (25)

The team continued to play slightly above .500 into early June, then had a very solid series in Washington against the Nationals. They won three out of four games, with Rizzo going 8 for 16. That included a two-homer game, along with another long drive in the same contest that was snared at the wall!

The month of July started brilliantly for the North Siders. Their 6-1 victory over the Mets in New York featured another stellar performance by Arrieta and the completion of a seven-game season sweep over the Mets.

According to the Cubs, the franchise hadn't swept a season series of at least that many games against an opponent since the very successful 1885 season. The team, known then as the Chicago White Stockings, compiled an unbelievable 87-25 record.

The Cubs split a significant four-game home series against the Cardinals just before the All-Star break. After losing the opener 6-0, they came back the next day to win a doubleheader 7-4 and 5-3. The second game featured a game-winning double by Addison Russell that twisted its way down the first base line and was barely fair when it crossed the bag.

The next night spelled heartbreak. Trailing early 4-0, the Cubs fought back and took the lead 5-4 on a bases clearing double by catcher Miguel Montero. It appeared that margin would hold until St. Louis shortstop Jhonny Peralta hit a dramatic two-out, two-run homer in the top of the ninth inning to put the Cardinals ahead for good, 6-5.

Overall, the Cubs concluded the first half of the season with a 47-40 record, and stood in third place in the National League Central, eight games behind the division leading Cardinals. They also were firmly situated, at the time, to get the second wild card spot in the season ending playoffs.

After the All-Star Game break, the team split a four-game series in Cincinnati, thanks largely to their two catchers at that time. With the Cubs on the verge of losing a second straight game to the Reds, rookie Kyle Schwarber hit a two-run homer in the ninth to send the game into extra innings, then won it with a solo blast.

The next day, veteran journeyman catcher Taylor Teagarden saved the Cubs from being swept in a doubleheader. His dramatic single in extra innings brought home the winning run.

Returning home for the start of a long home-stand, the Cubs were humiliated by last place Philadelphia. They not only were swept over the weekend, but had a no-hitter thrown against them by Cole Hamels. It was the first time in 50 years, since 1965, they were the victims of a no hit game on their home field by Hall of Famer Sandy Koufax. (26)

The next weekend, they journeyed 90 miles north to play at Milwaukee and Rizzo put on a hitting clinic. The first baseman made it four straight games with a home run with a three-run shot in the third inning to lead the Cubs to a 4-2 victory in the third game of the series over the Brewers..

"He's really on a roll and it's fun to watch," Cubs manager Maddon told the *Associated Press.* (27)

The slugger went 7 for 11 with three home runs in the first three games against the Brewers. He has hit 13 in his career against Milwaukee, the most against any opponent.

The Cubs wound up sweeping the entire four-game series, and then split a rain shortened two-game series in Pittsburgh before returning home to meet the San Francisco Giants, World Series winners in three of the last five years.

Just like the previous weekend in Milwaukee, the Cubs made mincemeat of the defending champion Giants, dominating the series with a four-game sweep.

It was a vitally important series in which Maddon benched Castro, his regular shortstop, and moved Russell there from second base. Chris Coghlin, who had primarily played in the outfield, was moved to second for the time being. This opened the gates for the possible move of Javier Baez back to his second base post, where he previously played for the Cubs, or even possibly Castro.

The winning continued at home as the Cubs swept yet another four-game set over the woebegone Brewers. The highlight wasn't the dominant Cubs hitting, although there was plenty of that, but a spectacular catch on a foul ball by first baseman Rizzo. He chased the pop-up along the first base line to where the tarpaulin is kept, jumped on it and stretched into about the third row to catch the ball. Incredible!

Two days later he hit a game-winning home run in a 6-5 win over the White Sox for the team's 8th straight victory. The streak reached nine before they were utterly stymied in the third game by Chris Sale.

Then the Detroit Tigers came to town for what proved to be a disastrous two-game hit-fest with the visitors winning 10-8 and 15-8.

According to the Elias Sports Bureau, this marked the first time since 1956 that Cubs' starting pitchers gave up three or more home runs in three consecutive games. And Lester was the victim in the 15-8 romp. (28)

The weekend, however, saw a complete reversal as the Cubs put together another four-game sweep, this time against the Atlanta Braves. They hit in the clutch and for power in each game. In fact, it was their fourth sweep of a four-game series in one season for the first time since 1945, when they last won the National League pennant.

This was followed by a journey to the West Coast, which started poorly, but ended with a dream performance in Los Angeles. On the last Sunday in August, before a national television audience, Arrieta was absolutely unhittable.

He threw a brilliant no-hitter against the Dodgers, as the Cubs won 2-0 thanks to a first inning home run by Bryant. Arrieta allowed only two baserunners, one reaching on an error and the other via a walk. He became the first Cubs pitcher to allow nary a hit since Carlos Zambrano's gem in 2008 and it was just the team's second no hitter in 43 years.

They came home and won four out of six over Cincinnati and Arizona which included another not to be forgotten monster shot by Bryant in the finale against the Diamondbacks. It was an unbelievable blast off the left field scoreboard, estimated by Statcast to have traveled 495 feet.

"I don't know if I've ever seen a ball hit that far. Good thing the board was there, otherwise it would still be flying," catcher Montero told the *Chicago Sun-Times*.

And Maddon added, "I think 495 feet is a misconception. It has to be farther than that. That ball was absolutely annihilated." (29)

That win enabled the Cubs to sweep the three-game series over the Arizonans and set the stage for their vital road trip, starting with three match-ups in St. Louis.

Lead-off batter Fowler sent an early message with a home run, then followed that with a two-run double an inning later as the Chicagoans were on their way to a 9-0 whitewash over their dreaded Mississippi River rivals. It was Cubs biggest shutout victory over the Cardinals since a 10-0 romp in September, 1981.

The teams split the next two games of the series with the Cubs holding off a late rally to win 8-5, then falling victim to a three-run eighth inning by the Cards in their 4-3 triumph.

A four-game weekend followed at Philadelphia, the team with the worst record in baseball, but the Cubs only could gain a split before heading to Pittsburgh.

They began with a doubleheader and after losing 5-4, Lester took matters into his own hands. He threw a complete game in a 2-1 win, dominating the Pirates' tough hitters.

The next night Arrieta took the mound seeking his 20th win. While that didn't happen, the Cubs still managed to eke out a 3-2 victory in 12 innings.

Closing in on both St. Louis and Pittsburgh in the Central Division with two weeks left in the regular season, the Cubs next returned home to host the always-tough Cardinals over the weekend.

Friday's game turned out to be the Starlin Castro show as the second baseman clubbed two home runs along with six RBIs in an 8-3 win. The second blast prompted thrilled fans to holler for a curtain call, to which he gladly obliged.

He was ecstatic afterwards and told the *Associated Press,* "I've played here six years now and that never happened before. This was my first time and I enjoyed it so much." (30)

Then on Saturday, the Cubs offense continued to flourish in a 5-4 win that featured homers from Soler and Bryant. It was a franchise-tying record for Bryant when he blasted his 25th round-tripper, equaling future Hall of Famer Billy Williams' team mark for round-trippers by a rookie.

Maddon continues to rave about Bryant's progress over the course of the season, telling the Sarasota *Herald Tribune,* "The adjustment he's made is totally night and day. Give the kid a lot of credit for being open-minded to the whole moment. He sought advice from hitting coach John Mallee who suggested several minor adjustments to his swing. There was a simple plan enacted, which has made a huge difference." (31)

It only took a few days for Bryant and Arrieta to excel once again, this time against the Cubs' favorite punching bag during the season, the Milwaukee Brewers.

Bryant slammed his 26th home run, breaking the team's rookie record for long balls in the same contest where Arrieta threw a complete game for his 20th win of the season. It was a 4-0 shutout win in which he allowed only three-hits to become the first Cub to win 20 since Jon Lieber accomplished the feat in 1991.

The huge weekend series brought the Pirates to Chicago and even though the Cubs dropped the first game, 3-2, they clinched their first trip to the post-season since 2008 when the San Francisco Giants lost that night to Oakland.

Now it was a matter of trying to overtake the Pirates to host the Wild Card game or, better yet, make a miracle run to overtake St. Louis to win the division.

The latter didn't happen as the Cardinals, despite numerous injuries, continued to come up with solid replacements and ultimately win over 100 games to capture the Central Division for the third consecutive year.

The Cubs kept winning with regularity. Arrieta nearly pitched another no-hitter, this time a perfect game into the seventh inning against the Pirates on a nationally televised game. Then they swept Cincinnati and entered the final weekend two games up on the Pirates with three to go.

Winning two out of three in Milwaukee, while the Pirates lost two out of three to the Reds would give the Cubs home field advantage in the upcoming wild card playoff game. If the teams wound up tied, the game would be played at Wrigley Field by virtue of the Cubs winning the season series.

They beat the Brewers, thanks to more incredible shutout pitching by Arrieta, for his 22nd win, and Hendricks, in the first two games. The Pirates, meantime, split their two games against the Reds, leaving Maddon's team just a game back going into the final day of the regular season.

The Cubs did win that regular season final 3-1 as Rizzo drove in his 100th and 101st runs of the year, the first time he's hit the century mark. It gave them 97 wins thus far with the playoffs about to start.

Pittsburgh's 4-0 shut out over the Reds ensured them the home field advantage in the upcoming wild card game. It was sure to be a classic match-up on the mound in the Steel City with Arrieta facing Gerrit Cole, who has 19 wins to his credit.

In summing things up about the Cubs great turnaround for the 2015 season, Maddon excitedly told *MLB.com*, "I often talk about how I feel fortunate to be here because all the heavy lifting was done prior to me coming here. They took a beating for a couple years doing the right thing and all of a sudden guys are playing like they are. It was a combination of all that. It's played out pretty good the first year. (32)

The wild card game in Pittsburgh was dominated by the Cubs from the start. Kyle Schwarber had a run-scoring single in the first, then added a long two-run homer in the third. Arrieta, meantime, continued his invincibility, throwing a complete game, 4-hit shutout in a 4-0 win, the team's first post-season victory in 12 years. He also added 11 strikeouts and even stole a base.

From there it was on to St. Louis. In all the years of the intense rivalry between the two teams, they had never met before in post-season play, until now!

Lester came through with another strong effort in game one, only to be outpitched by Cardinals standout John Lackey in their 4-0 win. The Cubs left-hander only gave up three runs in nearly eight innings on the mound while the Cubs managed just three hits for the entire contest.

Game 2 of the series featured a big Cubs uprising in the second inning on the way to a 6-3 win. They scored five unearned runs, thanks largely to two Cardinals errors and a home run by Jorge Soler. It equaled the most runs scored in one inning by a

Chicago team in a playoff game since 1989. Their bullpen was also dominant, shutting out the Cardinals for 4 1/3 innings.

Arrieta took the mound again in game three and while he wasn't at his best, he didn't have to be. The Cubs pounded out an all-time postseason record six home runs, by six different players, on a windy Wrigley night, leading to an 8-6 win.

From the top in the batting order, Fowler, Soler, Bryant, Rizzo, Castro and Schwarber each deposited a long ball into the seats in this unprecedented performance to move within one win of clinching the series. That's a long ball from each of the top six hitters, which has never happened before, until now.

The next day could bring about a conclusion to the series between these two long-time rivals and it didn't start out well for the Cubs, as the Cardinals touched home plate twice in the first inning.

That lead was short-lived when the Cubs put up four runs of their own, thanks largely to a three-run blast by Javier Baez. The Cardinals eventually tied the game and threatened to go ahead until Soler's brilliant throw from right-field nailed a runner at home plate in the top of the 6th.

Then it was Rizzo and Schwarber's turn to take matters into their own hands, each with a long solo homer, giving the Cubs a 6-4 win and a spot in the National League Championship series against the New York Mets. It is their first time to play for a trip to the World Series since 2003.

The victory also marked the first time in the long history of Wrigley Field (1916) that the Cubs had clinched a playoff series at home. It set off an hours-long celebration which started in the ballpark and eventually grew much larger through the Wrigleyville community. Long-time fans were utterly exuberant over the team's growing success.

"We've come full circle within a year, and it's kind of amazing to be in this particular moment with all this at stake. This is what you work for. Again, I'm really happy for the fans to be able to participate in this moment. I think it's fabulous," Maddon told *MLB.com*. (33)

Now it's onward to the next step and the hope of advancing to the World Series for the first time in 71 years.

The series opener, however, was not to be either the Cubs' or starter Lester's night. He gave up a home run to Daniel Murphy in the first, another blast by Travis d'Arnaud in the sixth and two more runs during his time on the mound as the Cubs lost 4-2.

Mets starter Matt Harvey held the Cubs in check, except for another long home run by Schwarber, which traveled over 460 feet.

Game two in the series marked the return of Arrieta, who told the *Chicago Tribune* that despite his heavy work load, he's ready and excited to go. "Obviously, there are certain things you can't control, but physically, my body feels great. There's some still some work for me to be done, and I don't think I've gotten to the end of my leash yet." (34)

Unfortunately, the first inning was a bad one for the Cubs' ace. He quickly gave up three hits and three runs, topped off again by another home run off the bat of Murphy. The Mets, behind pitcher Noah Syndergaard, won 4-1 to take a two game lead in the series that now heads back to Chicago.

Home, sweet, home as the Cubs took the field in search of the National League pennant for the first time since 2003 against Florida. This time they faced Mets right-handed flamethrower Jacob deGrom against Hendricks.

After the visitors scored a run in the top of the first, it was Schwarber again to the rescue with his fifth home run of the playoffs.

Murphy continued to be a huge pest for the Mets with a long ball of his own, the fifth consecutive game in which he's connected. Then the Cubs' Soler tied the game again at 2-2 with another homer into the center field bleachers.

The Mets got a gift in the sixth inning to take the lead when a strikeout turned into a wild pitch, enabling the go-ahead run to score from third for a 3-2 New York lead. They added two more in the seventh and made it hold up for a 5-2 win, and a 3-0 lead in the series. The Cubs now faced the monumental task of having to win four straight games to advance.

"It's not going to be easy," Maddon said after the game. "But it can be done." (35)

Right out of the gate, Cubs starter Jason Hammel faced big trouble and before the first inning was over, he had given up a three-run homer to Lucas Duda, along with a solo shot by d'Arnaud for a 4-0 Mets lead. They added more in the third, thanks again to

Duda with a two-run double, giving him five runs batted in.

The game then slowed down until Murphy slammed a two-run homer in the eighth, his major league record sixth consecutive playoff game with a long-ball and the final score was 8-3, sending the Mets to their first World Series since 2000.

The Cubs, from manager Maddon through the entire roster, were obviously disappointed, but still very excited over their wonderful season.

Rizzo was adamant in telling the *Chicago Tribune* this is just the beginning, "We set a tone for how we are going to be for a long time." (36)

Pitching standout Arrieta also told the *Tribune,* "I'm not big on outside expectations, but we accomplished a lot as a team. We won 97 games in a really competitive division with some experienced teams, and we played well from start to finish, and played better as our young players started to acclimate to this level and consistently have success." (37)

It was indeed a magical season and now onward to a busy off season of evaluating and determining what changes and / or additions are needed to move this exciting team to the next level.

White Sox in 2015

For the White Sox, the decade after their 2005 World Championship was a mixed bag, mostly mediocre and disappointing, except for the one division title. They did manage second place finishes in 2010 with 88 wins and again in 2012 with 85.

But they plodded their way through a very embarrassing 2013 campaign with 99 losses, the second worst season ever. Only 1976, with 106 setbacks, was worse.

New General Manager Rick Hahn, a longtime presence in the front office, and manager Robin Ventura, a former standout third baseman for the White Sox, as well as three other teams, brought in several new players with outstanding credentials.

First and foremost was Cuban slugger Jose Abreu, who had a great first season in 2014 with 36 home runs, 107 runs batted in and a .317 batting average. He was the unanimous choice for 2014 American League Rookie of the Year and played a key role in the team's improvement to a 73-89 record. (38)

His next season, in 2015, was also very impressive with 30 homers and 101 RBIs. That made him just the second player in major league history, along with the great Albert Pujols, to begin his career with back to back seasons with 30 or more homers and over 100 RBIs.

Hard-throwing left-handed pitcher Sale was a 12-game winner with a low earned run average in 2014 and added 13 more victories the following year. Center fielder Adam Eaton hit .300 in 2014, then batted .284 a year later and right-fielder Avasail Garcia, despite being injured for much of the year, showed some flashes of potential greatness despite having far too many strikeouts.

Many White Sox fans were calling for the team to trade him.

Prior to the start of 2015, they added former Cubs and Oakland pitcher Jeff Samardzija; right-handed closer David Robertson, a former New York Yankee; left handed reliever Zach Duke from Milwaukee and right handed late inning specialist Matt Albers from Houston; outfielder Melky Cabrera from Toronto and designated hitter-first baseman Adam LaRoche from Washington.

The White Sox opened their season by losing to a perennial nemesis, the Kansas City Royals. They were humiliated 10-1 and never had a chance.

Former Cub Samardzija's first regular season start in a Sox uniform was dreadful.   The only bright spot was a long home run by Abreu.

The White Sox ended up getting swept in that opening series and when Kansas City came to Chicago two and a half weeks later, it was a very testy series. Several batters were hit by pitchers, leading to a brawl and the eventual suspensions of players from each team, including both Sale and Samardzija, the White Sox best starting pitchers.

That was followed by tragedy in Baltimore where Samardzija became part of history. The team arrived there for a three-game series against the Orioles about the same time violent protests occurred around the city over the death of 25-year-old Freddie Gray while in police custody. His spinal cord was severed as he was transported to jail by police after being arrested.

The first two night games in the series were postponed and the third was re-scheduled for an afternoon contest on Wednesday, April 29th and would be played in Camden Yards with no audience. It was the first time in the long history of Major League

Baseball that a game was played with no fans in the stands.

Most members of the White Sox called the atmosphere "weird" and "different." "It was just a surreal environment," Manager Ventura told the *Chicago Tribune*. "I don't think we really want to play another one like this." (39)

And with good reason, Samardzija was the Sox starter against Baltimore's Ubaldo Jiminez and the game was over in the bottom of the first. A three-run homer by the Orioles Chris Davis opened up the floodgates in an 8-2 win for Baltimore. Unfortunately for Samardzija, he gave up all eight runs in five innings, six of them in the first.

Sox second baseman Micah Johnson said the glare of the unoccupied seats was distracting on defense. He could hear the TV announcers in the booths and the Orioles in their dugout. And he was self-conscious about his own vocal reactions to mistakes as he called out "no" and "my bad."

"I can't even compare it to anything, but it was definitely weird," Johnson said. "It's quiet. There's nothing going on. You hear everything. Obviously it was better for the Orioles than us today. It's not how baseball is supposed to be played." (40)

If the White Sox thought the corner would be turned in Minneapolis over the May Day weekend, they were sorely mistaken. In a four-game sweep, they were outscored 31-8, outhit 50-36, and out homered 5-0 by the Twins. The Sox did, however, "win" one category. Thanks to four errors on Sunday, they had six in the series to three for Minnesota.

After the weekend debacle, things picked up a bit when they returned home. They won four out of six match-ups against Detroit and Cincinnati.

The key win over the Tigers found them trailing 6-3 with two out in the eighth when White Sox bats exploded for six straight hits, including a game-tying three-run home run by Cabrera. Garcia eventually singled home the game-winner. The front office and manager Ventura had been promising an outburst like this for the entire season and it finally came.

Rookie Carlos Rodon, an All-American pitcher at North Carolina State University, who had been the number three overall draft pick when the Sox selected him the previous summer, was brilliant in his first-ever major league start against the Reds.

He pitched six strong innings - two earned runs, four hits, eight strikeouts –to beat Cincinnati 8-2 in the second game of a doubleheader.

Rodon, despite walking four, looked ready to assume a spot in the rotation, according to *Beachwood Reporter* correspondent Roger Wallenstein who wrote, "His breaking ball really moves, and his fastball was clocked as high as 98 on Saturday. His mound presence is far more mature than most 22-year-olds with just 34 innings of minor league experience." (41)

"When Carlos started at N.C.State in 2012, he simply didn't throw enough strikes," his college pitching coach Tom Holliday told *Collegiate Baseball* magazine.

"He wanted to throw 190 mph with his fastball, and he didn't understand the vital importance of command. We made several mechanical adjustments as we shortened his stride and made his mechanics more compact. All of a sudden, the light went on. He learned that he didn't have to reach all the way back and strike out everybody," Holliday explained. (42)

Like the Cubs did just before them, the White Sox also put together a six-game winning streak in mid-

May. It included a three-pack of wins during a weekend in Oakland, where they traditionally had played horrendous baseball in the A's outdated and poorly maintained ballpark.

It seemed that things were starting to come together, but not so fast. They came home to face Cleveland and Minnesota, two other teams against whom they've struggled mightily, and no surprise, they lost five out of seven, looking terrible in the process.

Things continued to decline in early June when they lost four out of six in back to back series against Texas and Detroit. Samardzija was dreadful again in a 15-2 drubbing to the Rangers and couldn't hold a three-run lead in a 6-4 setback to the Tigers.

With a few exceptions, consistency certainly wasn't a strong point for the team, both pitching-wise and at the plate.

One of those was the stellar pitching by Sale. He became the first pitcher in the team's long history to throw five consecutive games with 12 or more strikeouts, including 14 against Houston and 13 over Baltimore and Texas. That eventually translated into his becoming the second pitcher in major league history to strike out 10 of more batters in eight straight games, tying Pedro Martinez for the unlikely feat. (43)

To no one's surprise, Sale was named the American League Pitcher of the Month, a fitting honor considering his performance during June was one of the best months for a White Sox pitcher in franchise history.

He struck out 75 over 44 1/3 innings covering six starts in June, allowing 28 hits, eight walks and nine earned runs, finishing with a 2-2 record and a 1.83 ERA for the month. His 75 strikeouts stand as the most by any pitcher in any month since Nolan Ryan set the modern era record with 87 in June 1977 (STATS LLCS). (44)

"I go out and try to give my team a chance to win every time. That's really the main job as a starter, fill up innings and when you leave the game your team has a chance to win," Sale told *MLB com.* "That's the only thing I've put focus on. Filling up innings and leaving my team with a chance to win is all you can really ask for out of yourself." (45)

Despite his brilliance, the team floundered badly, losing 8 games in a row in mid-June. During four consecutive games within that disastrous time, the

Sox managed only four hits or fewer in each contest. That had never happened before in the team's more than century long existence.

Overall for the month, they had a sad record of 10-16. Things continued to deteriorate into early July.

Then out of nowhere, the team won 9 out of 12 games right before the All-Star break. That included a pair of games in St. Louis against the always tough Cardinals and taking three out of four at home over Toronto, featuring a game-winning homer by Eaton and a four-hit shutout in a 2-0 much improved Samardzija win. The Sox then traveled across town to Wrigley Field and took two out of three behind solid starts from Rodon and Sale.

Now the question was being asked all around town: Are the Sox on the verge of an upswing in the second half or is it still a floundering team that may be destined for last place?

The latter was clearly the case after the South Siders, playing at home, dropped three of four games to the first-place Royals, managing only 11 runs in those contests.

Unfortunately, Sale wasn't quite himself in the Sunday match-up, giving up four runs and 11 hits in six-plus innings. He struck out only six Royals as the White Sox went down 4-1. Recent call-up Tyler Saladino's first big-league home run in the ninth inning averted a shutout.

The following weekend there was suddenly magic in the air. Despite all the adversity and problems plaguing the team throughout the season, all of a sudden things started falling into place during a four-game series in Cleveland. Not only did they sweep the Indians on the road for the first time since 2005, there also was another big success story.

The pitching staff put together five consecutive games without walking a single batter. That hadn't happened in 43 years, since 1972!

In addition, the White Sox bats came alive, scoring 26 runs over the weekend. Rookie second baseman Carlos Sanchez had the first two home runs of his major league career.

The road trip continued to go well in Boston where they took the first three out of four games, to run up a 7-game winning streak and suddenly find themselves within reach of a wild card berth, despite the lousy season to date.

In one of the wins, they started out with back-to-back triples from Eaton and Saladino, marking the first time the White Sox opened with two triples since June 15, 1954, against the Philadelphia A's. It was accomplished on that date by shortstop Chico Carrasquel and legendary Hall of Fame second baseman Nellie Fox.

Cabrera was outstanding during the seven game streak with multi-hit efforts and at least one run driven home in each contest. He's the first White Sox player ever to achieve that combined impressive accomplishment.

The last White Sox player to have seven consecutive multi-hit games was outfield star Magglio Ordonez between July 22nd and 30th, 2003.

The win streak ended as abruptly as it began when they lost to an obscure knuckle ball pitcher in Boston on a night when Sale looked very shaky.

Then they returned home and lost 4 of 6 to the Yankees and Rays, with Sale miserable again against Tampa and Samardzija also bad versus New York and later when he faced Kansas City and the Cubs, compiling a 12.91 earned run average in those three losses.

In fact, he allowed 22 earned runs since July 31, the end of the trading deadline when there was strong speculation he would be dealt elsewhere for younger prospects.

What once appeared to be a hopeful year was now turning into a nightmare. They dropped another three-game series at Kansas City to go 0-6 for the season on the Royals' home turf.

Despite that abysmal showing, they bounced right back and swept the California Angels in Chicago, thanks to strong pitching by Sale, Rodon and veteran John Danks.

Next up: the red-hot Cubs, who embarrassed the South Side home team in the first two games before running into Sale's superb strikeout showcase. He fanned 15 batters over seven innings in a 3-1 win, his most ever in a game.

Regarding Sale, Ventura was enthusiastic, "I don't know, not too many times he's been better than that. He's had some that were close to it but right from the start of the game, when he strikes out the guys in the first inning, strikes out the side, you're feeling pretty good about it," he told *MLB.com*. (46)

In addition, Nate Jones, fresh off the disabled list, struck out the side in the 8th inning, giving the team a record total number of 18. The Sox and Cubs wound up splitting the season series at three games each.

The White Sox inconsistency continued though when they began a seven game West Coast road trip. They dropped three out of four in Anaheim against the same Angels they had just swept in Chicago. Their bats dried up and shut down in the first three contests, just like the drought plaguing much of the nation.

But in game four, they rang up eight runs and followed that up a night later with 11 men crossing the plate in Seattle. Sale continued his brilliance with 14 strikeouts in an 11-4 win. They split the next two games in the Emerald City before heading home.

At U.S. Cellular Field, there was more mediocrity. The Sox only could salvage one win on their home field over Boston, and then proceeded to split a four-game weekend gathering against the Mariners. It took an 11th inning game-winning single by infielder Saladino to bail out the final game and prevent the Sox from losing the season series to Seattle.

After dropping two out of three in Minnesota in very frustrating fashion, the Sox next headed to Kansas City, where they'd lost all six games played there this season.

But surprise! The South Side "Agony Boys" swept the series with relative ease. Pitcher Erik Johnson, a prospect who had failed badly in a previous call-up, was brought back again from Triple AAA and did well in the final game of the set. It was their fourth straight win!

Labor Day brought the Cleveland Indians to Chicago to face Sale on the mound. Even though he had an early 2-0 lead, he surrendered three solo home runs, two by longtime Sox nemesis Ryan Raburn, resulting in a 3-2 setback.

They went on to lose two of three to the Tribe and did the same in the next series when the Twins returned to Chicago.

Next came the Oakland Athletics and after winning the opener 8-7 in 14 innings, despite blowing a four-run lead in the ninth inning, the following night was disastersville for the team and especially Samardzija. He gave up 10 earned runs in just over three innings as part of a 17-6 drubbing, joining Brett Tomko (2003) and Jaime Navarro (1997) as the only pitchers in last 50 years to give up more than nine earned runs three times in one year.

Most interesting in this debacle was Ventura's decision to use position player Ramirez and utility infielder Leury Garcia to each pitch an inning, the eighth and ninth. It was the first time since 1902 when two White Sox position players, Sam Mertes and Frank Isbell, took the mound in the same game, according to the *Elias Sports Bureau*. Isbell was later a hero on the Sox 1906 World Series championship team.

The following night, another historic moment occurred when newly acquired Mike Olt, a former Cubs third baseman, hit a long home run in a 9-4 Sox win. It marked the first time ever in which a player hit a home run for each Chicago team during the same season.

"It's a nice accomplishment," Ventura told the *Chicago Sun-Times*. "I mean, both teams have been around for a long time. It is surprising that nobody's done that before, so I'm glad he did it here. I'm glad he got the second one here." (47)

After losing two out of three games over the weekend in Cleveland, the Sox found themselves one game out of the Central Division cellar, just ahead of Detroit with a four-game series next in the Motor City.

It started with a doubleheader sweep by the Sox. Samardzija, who had been 1-8 in his last nine starts, had a complete reversal of form in the game one. He was near perfection, throwing a one-hit complete game as the Sox won 2-0 and only needed 88 pitches from start to finish. The lone blemish was a bloop single in the fifth inning.

Game two was also good for the Sox with Johnson throwing six solid innings in a 3-2 victory.

As has been the case all too often during the season, the Sox proceeded to regress and lost the remaining games against the Tigers. The only bright spot came in the finale when Cabrera hit the 100th home run of his career in a 7-4 setback.

From there it was on to the bright lights of New York to meet the Yankees, a certainty to make the playoffs. Sale took center stage and once again made a critical mistake that resulted in a Carlos Beltran three-run homer as the Sox lost 3-2.

Sale did register his 1,000[th] career strikeout, and also moved to within two strikeouts for the season of tying White Sox legend "Big Ed" Walsh's 269 that occurred over a century ago in 1908.

The Sox managed to win only one of the remaining three games in the Big Apple, thanks to a strong pitching performance by Rodon. Overall, there was more ineptitude for the South Siders, who were unable to hit with men in scoring position, continually swung at some terrible pitches and committed very costly errors along the way that made life much easier for the Yankees.

When Kansas City next came to Chicago, all eyes were focused on Abreu. He had a chance to become the second player in major league history after three-time Most Valuable Player Albert Pujols to hit 30 home runs and drive in 100 during each of his first two seasons.

He needed just one home run and three RBIs to accomplish those lofty goals.

A run-scoring single in the Sox 4-2 win in the first game of the series brought him within two, then a 7th inning game-tying home run in the second contest gave him 30 for the year though the Sox lost 5-3.

The following night his two-run single off Luke Hochevar brought his RBI total to 101, fulfilling this wonderful accomplishment and putting him in a very exclusive club.

"All the guys are proud of him," Ventura told *MLB.com*. "It's special for a guy to be able to do that. This game has been around a long time and for someone to accomplish that just shows his character and dedication." (48)

"It's a big honor to see my name now along with Albert," Abreu said through a team interpreter. "He's one of the greatest players in the history of baseball." (49)

Sale was back on the mound the next night against Detroit and picked up 7 more strikeouts to surpass Walsh's 107 year old team record of 269 during a single season with a new mark of 274 whiffs!

He was ecstatic over this milestone and his team's 2-1 win.

"There's a lot of stuff going on. I couldn't really pitch until I got it and after that I settled in," Sale told *MLB.com*. "It was fun. It was a great experience, something I'll never forget. It's awesome, something that hasn't set in yet but I know what it means, I know what it is, I'm very thankful for it and appreciative of it." (50)

After wins against the usually tough Tigers over the last weekend, the Sox clinched fourth place in the American League Central, the second straight year they avoided the cellar.

It was also announced by General Manager Rick Hahn that Ventura would return in 2016 for his fifth season as the team's manager. That news was met with disappointment by many frustrated and discouraged long-time fans.

"If we didn't feel as an organization that Robin had the ability to be a championship caliber manager, he wouldn't be here," Hahn said. (51)

Overall the White Sox finished the season with a disappointing 76-86 record, far below what they, their fans and baseball connoisseurs envisioned. Sadly, it's now a matter of wait until next year.

"Even if you go with the guys that are here, we're better off now than we were at the beginning of the year as far as playing the game," Ventura told the *WGN radio.* "Hopefully those slow starts aren't repeated." (52)

Chapter 5 – Onward to 2016

After their huge success and playoff run of the previous year, the Cubs were very upbeat heading into 2016. The White Sox, on the other hand, were hopeful despite their terrible performances during many games in 2015.

But no writer or analyst predicted either of them to wind up as opponents in the World Series. Maybe the Cubs would play for a championship, but for the White Sox, a wild card spot into the playoffs was a pipe dream, at best.

The first three weeks of spring training quickly began to change many people's thinking about the two Chicago teams during the upcoming season.

"Spring training doesn't usually mean that much in terms of how teams will perform during the regular season," is what baseball experts often say. For the most part that's generally true.

Great New York Yankee teams over the years have often floundered about in the Florida Grapefruit League exhibition games, losing more games than winning. But once the bell rings, they're off and running to another solid campaign.

Many teams that have done well in spring training have turned right around and stunk once they begin playing for real.

In recent years, the White Sox have been very mediocre during the Arizona Cactus League games. Last season, as an example, they only won 11 games and lost 17. The Cubs fared somewhat better, finishing at .500.

Once the season began, however, both teams surprisingly sprinted out to substantial leads in their divisions. The ball clubs each started the season on the West Coast. The Sox won three out of four in Oakland and after 20 games, they were 15-5.

The Cubs weren't far behind at 14-6. They began by sweeping two interleague games against the Los Angeles Angels and took three out of four in Arizona. National media experts speculated the White Sox start wouldn't last long. .

But it continued, by the time they had played 40 games, the Sox were a remarkable 24-16 and the Cubs even better at 28-12.

"I was thrilled to see those strong starts by both of our teams," recalls Jeff O'Fallon, less than a half-hour before the first pitch of this amazing all-Chicago World Series.

He continues talking with his new-found married friends, Katie Sorenson and Tom Buchanan and their soon-to-be born addition.

Katie let out a yelp and quickly says, "I'm OK, it's just our little guy or gal anxious to see daylight and watch this big game. It's been so active down there I can't help but think I'll wind up delivering early. I certainly hope not because I certainly want to see every one of these World Series games."

By mid-May, the White Sox and Cubs were the talk of baseball, amid speculation of something happening in October which hadn't occurred in 110 years.

The White Sox wound up the American League Central season with 90 wins while the Cubs were even better. They captured the National League Central with 105 victories, by far the most combined total number of wins during the regular season for the Chicago teams.

Yet, in the minds of many, this was also shaping up in a similar way to 1906, with the Cubs so dominant and the White Sox appearing to be a modern day version of "the hitless wonders."

As for the four traditional inter-league games between the teams, no surprise that they split the series, with each team winning two. Lester, who had dominated the White Sox for years as a member of the Boston Red Sox, continued that trend.

He shut out the Sox at Wrigley with a five-hit complete game 4-0 win and even hit a two-run double. He had long been considered one of the worst hitters in the history of major league baseball.

Sale also won a game against the Cubs by a 4-1 margin. He pitched into the eighth inning, allowing just six hits.

What thrilled him the most, he'll gladly tell you, was the home run he hit in the game at Wrigley where he parked a Ned Grabineau change-up out of the ballpark onto Sheffield Avenue.

But those were merely regular season games, much less significant than the World Series.

Each team had a strong candidate for Most Valuable Player in their respective league. White Sox first baseman-designated hitter Jose Abreu literally pounded the cover off the ball while nearly winning the American League Triple Crown with 42 home runs, 144 runs batted in and a solid .337 batting average. Seattle's second-baseman Robinson Cano had a slightly higher average at .340.

Cubs third baseman Kris Bryant continued his sensational rookie year numbers, walloping 48 more home runs and driving in 128 while batting .287. He hit 31 of those long-balls in the friendly confines of Wrigley.

In terms of pitching, the teams again were equally exceptional. The White Sox so-called southpaw strike-out slingers, Sale and Rodon, combined to win 39 games. Sale, with his oft-described "funky" delivery, had 22 victories while Rodon added 17 more. Erik Johnson had another 15 and came into his own as one of the league's top right handers. Sale is considered the favorite to win the league's Cy Young award, which will be announced after the World Series.

Relief pitcher David Robertson had 44 saves in his second year with the White Sox, a considerable improvement over the 34 games he closed out the previous year.

The Cubs had another monster year from Arrieta with 23 wins. He and Los Angeles Dodger perennial great Clayton Kershaw are considered top choices for the Cy Young in the National League. In addition, Cub left-hander Lester added 18 more victories and right-hander Hendricks had a strong season, with 16 wins. Their strong closer, Hector Rondon, added 38 saves.

To no one's surprise, Sale and Arrieta are selected by their managers to start game one of this classic World Series. Each had four wins thus far during the playoffs.

Sale beat Toronto twice in the first round, by 4-0 and 8-3 scores. In the second round for the American League title, he bested Seattle's Felix Hernandez 1-0 in a classic duel, then won 7-5 in one of his less than stellar performances.

Arrieta defeated the New York Mets' standout Mike Harvey by 2-0 and 5-2 scores. In the National League championship series, he first threw a two-hit shutout to beat the San Diego Padres 4-0, and then was dominant again in an 8-2 victory.

"I can't believe both teams blew through their series so far. Each team is 7-1 overall right now and if one of them sweeps the World Series, they'll be 11-1. Only two teams have ever done that, the White Sox in

2005 and the Yankees several years before them," Tom Buchanan says.

"Don't worry about that. These teams are so evenly matched, neither one is going to sweep the other," Jeff quickly replies.

Both O'Hare and Midway Airports are incredibly busy during the few days leading up to the start of the series. Thousands of former Chicagoans and those who had never lived here get off airplanes and trains feeling a great sense of Windy City pride and want to be a part of it, even if they aren't able to get a ticket to any of the games.

The pre-game ceremony features a cacophony of sounds from every corner of U.S. Cellular Field. Bands are blaring out many different tunes, several singers perform as part of the festivities and there mostly is an unbelievable buzz among the thousands of fans who show up long-before the 7:10pm scheduled first pitch.

The stadium is adorned with decorations. Traditional baseball World Series banners and bunting adorn the outfield walls and are also seen elsewhere throughout the place.

Chicago Mayor Rahm Emanuel is about to throw out the first of several "first pitches" being delivered primarily by politicians and performers, each drawing a large cheer, a couple of those more like the "Bronx jeer" variety.

Ticket prices for this World Series are beyond outrageous, ranging from $5,000 for prime box seats to nearly $500 just to be there, with either bleacher or second-deck locations far, far away from the field. Those are just the listed prices. By the time some of these tickets are re-sold several times, the prices could easily be double or triple those amounts.

Compare that with the 1906 White Sox-Cubs World Series where box seats were $2 and the bleachers went for a whopping 50 cents!

"You could just walk up on game day and buy a ticket then," Jeff explains. "Of course the game was just in its baby stages. My grandfather used to tell me the stories he heard from his grandfather, my great-great-great grandfather, on how the game grew to a point where now the sky's the limit in terms of ticket prices."

Chapter 6 – Game 1, October 21, 2016 World Series

Starting pitchers Chris Sale and Jake Arrieta are warming up, getting ready for the start of the first Chicago crosstown World Series in 110 years. That's a whopping 1,320 months, or 5,720 weeks, or roughly 40,150 days! Imagine that!

Longtime White Sox field announcer Gene Honda introduces the renowned James Cornelison to sing the National Anthem in his resounding, booming voice. He's been entertaining sellout crowds at the Chicago Blackhawks home hockey matches in the United Center for the past eight years. And when he's not doing that, he's busy with his primary role as a tenor vocalist with the Chicago Lyric Opera.

His performance on this chilly night nearly raises the roof beams along the first and third base lines and now it's truly time to begin, despite a threat of a big storm heading directly toward the Windy City.

Honda next announces Cubs leadoff batter, centerfielder Dexter Fowler, a .273 hitter during the regular season with 38 stolen bases and a good ability to get on base. He became a Cubs fan-favorite during the first week of the 2015 season. That's when he almost single-handedly won two games in Denver over the Colorado Rockies, one with a dramatic two-run home run with two out in the ninth inning and the other when he hit two triples.

The standing room only crowd at U.S. Cellular Field is in a state of euphoria as Sale gets set to deliver the first pitch at exactly 7:11pm on Tuesday, October 21st amid gusty, chilly winds and occasional snow flurries. People are bundled up in layers of clothing and ski parkas.

The left-hander winds up, goes into his rockem-sockem funky delivery and throws a fastball high and tight that requires Fowler to nearly do an adagio dance to get out of the way in a big hurry. But veteran home plate umpire Moe East says the pitch nicked him and points toward first base. Fowler heads toward the base and also glances out toward the pitchers' mound in anger as Sale holds his hands to one side, and gestures he's sorry that pitch got away from him.

Cubs fans who were able to get their hands on difficult to get tickets to this match-up at U.S. Cellular

Field let out a long round of boos, only then to be out-booed by nearly 37,000 White Sox fans on hand.

"What a crazy way to begin this long-awaited World Series," Jeff yells out to Katie, Tom, their soon to be born baby and anyone else within earshot.

Once the surprising start to the game settles in, Sale quickly throws two strikes past right fielder Jorge Soler. On the third pitch, which is a ball, Fowler takes off running and clearly beats the throw from White Sox catcher Timmy Vlessen. That puts a man in scoring position before a single out has been registered.

Soler strikes out swinging on the next pitch. That brings up first-baseman Anthony Rizzo, who has enjoyed a career year with a .308 batting average, 32 homers and 108 RBIs.

He wastes little time lining a hard single to center fielder Adam Eaton, who grabs it on the first bounce and fires a perfect throw to catcher Vlessen to tag out Fowler before he could ever touch home plate.

It happens so fast, Rizzo doesn't have time to even think about advancing to second base. Next up is Bryant, known affectionately as the "Wrigley Wrecker" since he hit 34 four-baggers at his home field during the season.

"Come on, Kris. Hit like you did against the Sox during the regular season," Katie yells out. She isn't kidding. The third-base slugger batted .350 in the four games against the South siders, including three homers, one off of Sale.

But not this time as he hits a soft pop-up to veteran shortstop Alexei Ramirez to end the top of the first.

"Now it's our turn," Tom leans over and whispers in Katie's ear. "They'll get two or three runs here off of Arrieta," he boldly predicts.

Eaton strides to the plate amid loud applause for his perfect throw home from center-field. He takes the first two pitches, for a strike and ball, and then lashes into pitch number three with a fury, sending the ball deep into right-center field as the crowd lets out a loud cheer.

"Oh, my God. He caught it!" Katie yells out as Fowler repays Eaton for the brilliant throw home in the top of the first, with a diving catch near the warning track.

"That for certain would have been a triple," O'Fallon says. "And might have been an inside the park home run. God, my great-great-great granddad would have had a field day describing that catch in the newspaper."

Left-fielder Melky Cabrera is up second and lunges after the first pitch with no success. He hits a weak pop-up in foul territory that is grabbed by first baseman Rizzo.

Next to the plate comes Abreu, who, despite his great season, has struggled mightily against Arrieta in White Sox-Cubs games. He is only 1 for 7 in the two games against the hard-thrower and his one hit was a weakly hit chopper down the third base line.

The poor performance continues when the White Sox slugger takes a very weak swing at a ball down and in, striking out on four pitches.

Sale and Arrieta pitch to near-perfection through the fourth inning. The game remains scoreless. The only hit for the White Sox is a second inning single into center field by Ramirez.

The Cubs have just the first inning single by Rizzo to show up in the hit column.

Each pitcher has thrown 47 pitches heading into the fifth, or just under 12 an inning, which is considered an excellent number.

Sale starts the new frame by throwing two quick strikes to slow-running catcher Miguel Montero. The next pitch is hit very hard down the left-field line for a double and now it will be interesting to see how the Cubs play it.

Will manager Joe Maddon have shortstop Addison Russell try a sacrifice bunt to get Montero to third and give designated hitter Chris Denorfia, batting ninth, a good chance to knock him in? Or will he let the .268 hitter swing away and try to at least hit the ball to the right hand side so there may still be a chance for the runner to advance?

Sale's first pitch is a hard slider that Russell takes a mighty swing at and misses. After a ball, Russell goes into a bunting stance and hits a weak pop foul that White Sox catcher Vlessen, a top Rookie of the Year candidate, chases after to his left and makes a diving stab to grab it.

By this time Montero is already half way to third, so Vlessen's toss to second baseman Carlos Sanchez doubles him off. Two pitches later, Denorfia grounds out harmlessly ending the half-inning.

Both pitchers continue to excel, keeping the game scoreless with only a total of three hits, two for the

Cubs and one for the Sox. Sale and Arrieta's solid
pitching brings back memories of "Three Finger"
Brown and "Big Ed" Walsh in the 1906 all-Chicago
World Series.

"My grandfather used to tell me what his granddad
told him about how dominant those pitchers were 110
years ago when he was covering the World Series for
the *Chicago Gazette*," Jeff O'Fallon yells out. "Now
we're all seeing this same thing all over again, more
than a century later. It's absolutely unbelievable!"

The Cubs don't waste any time mounting a
significant threat in the sixth inning. Leadoff batter
Jorge Soler finds a pitch to his liking and sends it high
and deep to left fielder Cabrera, who moves back and
under it near the fence. He leaps and nearly comes
up with the catch but the ball caroms off the top of the
wall and away from the closest Sox players. By the
time shortstop Ramirez gets to the ball in the outfield,
Soler moves into third base with a stand-up triple.

Javy Baez, the leftfielder, is next to bat. After taking
two pitches for balls, he hits a high popup into short
left field that Cabrera catches. Soler bluffs and takes
a few steps toward the plate, but quickly retreats
when he sees the throw home is right on target.

Montero then comes to the plate and goes into a bunting stance for a likely suicide squeeze play. But Sale throws the pitch down and in, making it virtually unbuntable, yet still is called a strike.

Just after that pitch, a gigantic bolt of lightning and a deafening clap of thunder are seen and heard. It sends a murmur of fear through the standing room only crowd of nearly 40,000.

There has been strong speculation of rainy days ahead. Legendary WGN-TV weathercaster Tom Skilling warned of possible rain delays during the all-Chicago World Series. A big, slow moving front, he said, is coming in over the plains states, heading straight for northern Illinois, with heavy rain accumulations expected in the Chicago area.

Umpires quickly check with the grounds crew after the unscheduled sky show to make sure they are ready to get the tarp on the field if and when the skies unload.

Once they are convinced everyone is set to act, if needed, the game continues.

Montero, the catcher, takes two pitches for a strike and a ball, then swings late and grounds out to third baseman Tyler Saladino, ending the threat and the game remains scoreless.

Raindrops begin falling between the top and bottom of the sixth as the rumble of thunder is heard in the distance, along with more flashes of lightning.

Vlessen, the White Sox catching phenom, hits Arrieta's first pitch into left center field for a double.

"He's going to be great and he's already doing real good right now for a kid just called up to the majors," lifelong Sox fan Tom Buchanan shouts out while hugging his pregnant wife.

Vlessen indeed has been a surprise for the South siders. He was drafted in the 21st round two years earlier out of California State - East Bay in Hayward, a Division 2 school. Once considered a possible mid-level National Football League draft pick as a linebacker, he also played baseball in college and greatly improved as a catcher over the years.

He started with Great Falls, Montana, in the Rookie League the previous summer and tore the cover off the ball, batting .374 with 8 home runs in just 6 weeks before being promoted to the advanced Class A team in Winston-Salem, North Carolina. There he not only continued to hit, but also threw out 12 of 20 attempted base stealers.

Going into spring training in Arizona this season, plans were to have him start in April with the Class AA team in Birmingham, Alabama. But after the display of hitting and defense he showcased in Glendale, the White Sox brass opted to have him start at Class AAA in Charlotte, North Carolina.

And he didn't disappoint anyone. By mid-June he was hitting .295, with 6 homers and 40 runs batted in and had thrown out 60 per cent of base runners trying to steal. His efforts were soon rewarded with a ticket to the major league team where he hit .253 with 4 home runs and solid defense behind the plate. The team hadn't seen a catching prospect like this in years.

The rain begins to pick up in intensity as second baseman Sanchez steps to the plate. Arrieta walks around on the mound, seeming to stall and hoping the umpires will call a halt to play with a relatively short weather delay. But it isn't raining hard enough yet.

Sanchez moves into a sacrifice bunt stance, making an effort to get Vlessen to third with just one out. Bunting has been a major shortcoming of the White

Sox in recent years, but Sanchez has been somewhat successful during the season, advancing runners via the bunt 12 times.

Only four times in the last 50 years has a White Sox player led the American League in sacrifice bunts. Outfielder Juan Pierre had 19 in 2011, as did infielder Joey Cora in 1993. Bucky Dent put down 23 sacrifices in 1974 and Don Buford had 17 in 1966. (53)

On the third pitch to him, Sanchez does get down a reasonably good bunt toward first baseman Rizzo who fakes a throw to third but instead tags the batter for the inning's first out as Vlessen slides into third.

When Eaton steps into the batter's box, the skies unload with a vengeance. Rain comes down in buckets, accompanied by lightning and thunder. In addition, the water almost immediately begins to cascade off the rooftop into the stands. The crowd heads en masse toward the exits, seeking cover on the concourses at each level.

"It's raining so hard, I can't imagine they'll be able to resume playing this game tonight," Buchanan says. "Look, the infield is already nearly underwater."

The grounds crew, led by third-generation crew chief Roger Bossard, regarded by many as a master of the manicured lawn and garden as well as having the ultimate green thumb, is seriously challenged. He and his crew struggle mightily just to get the huge tarpaulin on the field during the downpour and ferocious wind.

"This is without a doubt one of the most difficult challenges we've ever faced in my many decades as a groundskeeper," says Bossard, affectionately known as 'The Sodfather.' "That includes many years of helping my grandfather and father before I became the crew chief."

The situation poses a potentially big problem for Major League Baseball if the game doesn't resume on this suddenly turbulent night.

Rules involving rain delays and/or postponements in the World Series or playoff games changed dramatically in 2008 during the Tampa Bay-Philadelphia World Series. That's when then-commissioner Bud Selig determined that no team would be allowed to win a series game, or clinch the series, in a rain-shortened contest.

In that case, game 5 was suspended after the top of the sixth inning on October 28th. Two days later after the rains stopped and everything had dried, play resumed and the Phillies won the game 4-3, wrapping up their second World Series championship, four games to one. That's a very small number of titles for a team that's been around since 1885. They also have won only seven National League pennants.

As for ticket distribution for the continuation of the suspended game, fans who came back two days later were able to use the same ticket, listed as game 5, for admission since it was still the continuation of that game.

Those tickets included a rain check stub, and replacement tickets were not issued. Selig promised to "bend over backwards to be sensitive" to the fans of Philadelphia lauding them as "tremendous."

He said at the time, "These fans obviously came and bought tickets for a night game, so they deserve to come back and see a night game. Yes, it will be the same starting time, whether it's Tuesday night or Wednesday night or Thursday night or whenever." (54)

The most historic postponement of a World Series was the 1989 Bay Area match-up between the San Francisco Giants and Oakland Athletics. The start of Game 3 was delayed ten days, the longest stoppage of play in World Series history.

That was the result of the devastating Loma Prieta earthquake, which hit as 62,000 fans were settling into their seats at 5:04pm on October 17th in Candlestick Park. The 6.9 magnitude temblor resulted in 63 deaths and nearly 3,800 injuries, many of them very severe.

Of the fatalities, the majority occurred in Oakland where a portion of the double-deck Nimitz Freeway collapsed and pancaked, crushing and killing many innocent victims in their vehicles.

The epicenter of the earthquake was 10 miles northeast of Santa Cruz in a section of the San Andreas fault and the overall amount of damage caused by this tragedy was nearly $6 billion.

When the series was eventually resumed, the Athletics, who won the first two games before the delays, also won the next two. That completed a four-game sweep over a span of 14 days.

Coincidentally, the Giants were also involved in the second longest World Series in 1962 against the New York Yankees. The reason it dragged on forever that time was stormy weather and continuous downpours on both the West and East Coasts.

It took 13 days to complete the seven-game series, which the Yankees won for their 20th overall championship at that time. But it didn't come easy. They took the decisive seventh game 1-0 in San Francisco after Giants slugger Willie McCovey hit a screaming line drive into the glove of Yankees second baseman Bobby Richardson with the bases loaded with Giants players in the ninth inning.

Overall, the Giants had a higher cumulative batting average and lower earned-run average, thanks to stingy pitching, blasted more home runs, triples and doubles, yet still lost the Series. It devastated the City by the Bay.

The rain continues to drench U.S. Cellular Field on this opening night of the World Series. Upstairs in the owner's box and executive suites, phone calls, e-mails and tweets are plentiful. What is likely to happen, many wonder, in the strong likelihood this game is suspended and forced to be continued tomorrow or two days from now?

A look at the field quickly says no way this game can be resumed tonight and maybe not even tomorrow. Besides the large build-up of water on the tarp, there are plenty of water holes, almost mini lakes, accumulating throughout the outfield.

Radar screens show nothing but red and orange masses covering the Chicago area and stretching as far west as Des Moines, Iowa. Forecasters are projecting heavy rain and very high winds to continue for the next 24 hours.

The situation has prompted local weathercasters to compare this storm with the worst one ever seen in and around the Chicago area. That occurred on July 23rd of 2011 when 6.86 inches drenched the area and caused a massive traffic jam around O'Hare Airport. Traditionally October is one of the least rainy months of the year, with an average of 3.15 inches. That much likely fell so far with this gully washer.

After an hour-long delay, public address announcer Honda tells the few thousand fans remaining in the stands and many more on the concourses that tonight's game is being suspended at the point where it stopped. It will be resumed either tomorrow (Wednesday) or Thursday night depending on the weather conditions.

"An announcement will be made tomorrow morning at 10am on all media as to when the game will continue. Make sure you keep your tickets from tonight to ensure your being able to attend the continuation of this game," Honda continues.

"In addition, the ballpark and concession stands will remain open for at least two more hours, until 1 am, because of the adverse and dangerous conditions being experienced throughout the area," Honda tells the crowd. "Chicago Police and Major League Baseball urge you not to drive on the flooded expressways unless absolutely necessary."

"Wow," says Jeff O'Fallon. "I've never heard an announcement like that at a ballpark in all my years of covering sports events. I can't even imagine what my great-great-great grandfather would be saying now if he were here and heard something like that over a PA system."

Furthermore, ushers with hand-held, battery powered megaphones are scattered throughout U.S. Cellular Field making similar announcements and a large contingent of security personnel have started to appear on the concourses where thousands have gathered.

"We're cursed. The man upstairs doesn't want there to be a White Sox-Cubs World Series, no matter what anyone says," Buchanan shouts loudly to anyone who would listen to him amid the large groups gathered throughout the ballpark.

Both the Cubs and White Sox radio announcers on WSCR-AM (670) and WLS-AM (890) are strongly speculating about what might happen.

By this time, CBS newsradio stations WBBM-AM (780) and WCFS-FM (105.9) are also providing non-stop coverage of every imaginable aspect of the storm and its resulting flooding. Nearly six inches have fallen so far at Midway Airport in just under two hours, breaking numerous existing records and the rain is still coming down in torrents.

"Please stay off both expressways and surface streets, unless absolutely necessary," the radio voice pleads. "We're now also beginning to get a long list of school closings for tomorrow throughout the area. We're in the process of posting them on our website, so please check there or with the school district in your area."

We've also confirmed with the National Weather Service that this is at least the fourth worst storm in the city's history, surpassing the 5.63 inches that fell on August 2nd of 1885. That's 131 years ago!" the radio voice proclaims. (55)

"I guess we'll have to wait until our next meeting to tell you more about the 1906 series and the characters who inhabited both teams. Be careful getting home. The streets will be a total mess and the drivers will be distracted and disoriented," continues Jeff.

Chapter 7 – Game 1 Continuation
October 23, 2016 World Series

Daybreak on Wednesday brings a continuation of more rain, not quite as heavy, but still very steady and visible, with no exact idea from weathercasters when it might stop.

Live shots on early morning television newscasts show the field looking more like a big lake. The only thing missing are piers, boats and a raft for diving. This despite a very sophisticated drainage system that grounds crew chief Roger Bossard helped design and install when the ballpark opened in 1991.

At 10 am baseball Commissioner Rob Manfred addresses the media while holding a large umbrella from behind home plate and issues a short but quite succinct statement.

"As you can clearly see, it's still raining fairly hard, not nearly as badly as that incredible storm last night, but still a significant amount. What has us most concerned is the amount of water on the field.   So tonight's game is canceled but as long as the rainfall isn't as severe as it was last night, we should be able to play tomorrow night at 7:10 pm Central time," the commissioner explains. "We have every reason to believe the field will be in excellent shape by that time. Roger Bossard is one of the very best anywhere."

"We also have determined that the traditional day off scheduled for Thursday will be eliminated and the series will proceed on a daily basis through game five. Obviously, no travel days are needed since this series is being played in the same city. We'll see where we are after game five, if there's a need for more games," he concludes.

Now the pressing question to managers Maddon of the Cubs and Ventura of the White Sox becomes which pitchers would start the remainder of the suspended game? Should it be a regular starting pitcher, or perhaps a middle-inning relief pitcher? Since Arrieta and Sale each threw nearly 90 pitches, it's a virtual certainty that neither of them will come back for the conclusion.

Later that morning, both managers refuse to tip their hand as to which pitchers will start the delayed game. Perhaps Jon Lester of the Cubs, generally considered their number 2 behind Arrieta and Chris Rodon of the

White Sox, their second best hurler after Sale, or perhaps a resident of the bullpen?

The sun finally comes out by noontime and it is now a matter of hoping the bright rays on the field, along with Bossard's genius as a groundskeeper, will have the field in perfect condition by Thursday night. He is very optimistic.

By 7pm Wednesday, reports are circulating that Nate Jones, a hard-throwing White Sox right-handed reliever, may resume the game for his team, but no word yet on the Cubs situation.

Jones made his Major League debut in 2012 with the Sox, pitching out of the bullpen in middle relief. He had a great season, putting together an 8-0 record with a very respectable 2.39 earned run average (ERA) in 65 games.

He went 4-5 the following year, recording a 4.15 ERA in 70 appearances. Jones lost much of the 2014 season to serious injuries and never retired a batter. He appeared in two games, faced five hitters and gave up two hits, three walks and four runs with an ERA of infinity.

Jones eventually underwent both back surgery on May 5th and Tommy John surgery on July 29th. He started the 2015 season on the 60-day disabled list in an effort to continue recovery from both surgeries.

"Nate's been throwing the ball very well the past few months and I think he'll do well picking up the game at this point," says Ventura.

Thursday morning is beautiful. Not only is the sun shining, but the temperature on this fall day is already in the 60s. A look at the field makes one wonder if it actually had rained with such strength two nights earlier.

At 10am, Maddon announces that number four starter Jason Hammel will indeed be the Cubs pitcher in the bottom of the sixth inning.

"I feel very confident that Jason will do a great job here for however long we need him on the mound and then come back later in the series as a starter," the Cubs skipper says.

Hammel warms up for the Cubs. He's a steady and consistent right-hander who they acquired in a trade with Baltimore in 2014, then sent to the Oakland A's as part of a big mid-season deal and eventually re-signed again as a free agent. He has a solid repertoire of pitches and can be extremely deceptive with his delivery, as his 14 wins during the season indicate.

That, of course, throws a monkey wrench into the planned pitching match-ups for the remainder of the series and all the analyzing that went with them. It will certainly put a different perspective on each game.

Nice weather continues into early evening as the field dries out. When players from both teams take the field later that afternoon, conditions are ideal.

Soon it is time to again "play ball" with Adam Eaton stepping back into the batter's box. It's scoreless with one out and a man on third in the bottom of the sixth inning. The stands are completely packed again, along with at least 3,000 more standees.

Hammel's first pitch is a strike on the inside corner. A sacrifice bunt squeeze play seems doubtful here, because Vlessen is a slow runner. Not tortoise-like, as is the case with many catchers, but not exactly a speed-demon, either.

Eaton next takes a ball on a pitch where Hammel glares at home plate umpire East, thinking it is a strike.

After two more balls, and a 3-1 count, Eaton has a "hitterish" look on his face, hoping this pitch will be right in his comfort zone. But Hammel fools him with an off-speed slider for strike two.

After fouling off a couple more pitches, Eaton lets a pitch sail past him, obviously low for ball four, now putting runners on first and third.

Up steps Melky Cabrera, the 32-year-old veteran left fielder who has had a good season, batting .283. A one-time frequent .300 hitter, he's not quite as solid as in previous seasons, but is still very capable, which he immediately proves by slashing a double down the first-base line. That scores both Vlessen and hard-charging Eaton from first base, giving the White Sox a 2-0 lead.

Hammel is visibly very angry and upset. He stomps around the mound as White Sox fans begin yelling "Let's go White Sox" in harmony while Abreu readies to take his place in the batter's box. The first pitch is low and grounded to shortstop Russell who quickly fires the ball to third to get Cabrera who is running, perhaps unwisely, on the play.

Jones takes the mound for the top of the seventh, first facing lead-off hitter Fowler who hits the second pitch back through the middle for a single to center field. Left-fielder Baez is next and he also wastes no time, also hitting the first pitch hard on a line, but right to shortstop Ramirez. Fowler, who starts to run at the crack of the bat, quickly retreats and gets back to first base in time.

That brings up Rizzo who hits the fourth pitch thrown to him into left field for a single, putting runners on first and third.

White Sox fans throughout their home ballpark already are beginning to loudly question Ventura's decision to have Jones start the inning, instead of going with Rodon, the usual number two starter.

"What the hell is that idiot Ventura doing? Of course, in a game like this, you come back with a proven starting pitcher. Everyone in the ballpark knows that. Look how Maddon is playing it by starting Hammel?" questions a fan sitting behind Buchanan.

"Yeah, but he gave up two runs and Jones can still get out of this mess with a double play," he replies.

Jones also is rattled with the two men on base, only one out and slugger Bryant stepping up to the plate. The first pitch is much to the batter's liking and he sends it soaring high in the air and very deep down the left field line.

The only question here: fair or foul? The ball seems to take forever to come down and when it finally does, nearly 450 feet away, it's just a few feet foul.

Cubs fans are now shouting loudly as Jones gets a new ball from Vlessen and goes back into his stretch. This time he chooses a slow curve-ball, which fools Bryant and results in an awkward swing. After two balls, the slugger flies out to Avasail Garcia in right field, scoring Fowler it make it a 2-1 game.

Jones eventually gets out of the inning and Sox fans rise for the seventh inning stretch and a rousing version of "Take Me Out to the Ballgame," sung by 1960s rock group The Buckinghams, all lifelong residents of the Windy City. The band, formed in 1966, had several big hits over the years, including "Kind of a Drag," which reached number one on the *Billboard* chart.

Hammel is virtually unhittable in the bottom of the seventh, retiring the Sox on just nine pitches, including two strikeouts. Onward to the eighth, with left-hander Zach Duke now taking the hill for the home team.

The southpaw has been above average in his two seasons playing on the south side since being signed as a free agent after previously playing for five other major league teams. He began his career as a starter for the Pittsburgh Pirates, but eventually found his way into the bullpen with good success.

"As long as he keeps his pitches low, Zach should do alright tonight," Buchanan says. "But once he throws pitches closer to the waist, big trouble. I remember that game in Milwaukee last year where the Sox made a big comeback to tie it 7-7, then Duke gave up two home runs in the eighth to (Elian) Herrera and (Khris) Davis. The game was over. He just can't let that happen."

Baez leads off the inning and grounds out to third, followed by pinch hitter Kyle Schwarber's fly out to center fielder Eaton.

That brings up shortstop Russell, who weakly swings at two pitches around his ankles and can only stir up air.

But he then takes two balls and fouls off four more. Another ball follows, then three additional fouls, making this a 12-pitch at bat. The 13th toss from Duke is a very unlucky one. Russell sends it deep to left field, appearing at first to be a routine fly ball. But as the wind carries it farther and farther toward the corner, Cabrera is running out of room. It hits off the foul pole just above the wall for a home run.

Katie lets out a wailing yelp that could almost be heard all the way to Lake Shore Drive and hugs her husband, the huge White Sox fan, who has the most anguished look imaginable on his face.

She also grabs her stomach, letting out another yelp on a much lower level, but quickly says she isn't going into labor. It's just a sudden pain from the excitement.

Now the game is tied 2-2, and the Cubs have their number three starter on the mound. Hammel continues to look very sharp in the bottom of the eighth, recording two more strikeouts in another 1-2-3 inning.

On to the ninth and David Robertson, the regular White Sox closer, takes the mound. He rarely pitches more than one inning in each appearance. There have been some exceptions, but it's doubtful if Ventura would have him go any longer.

Robertson has been one of the better acquisitions for the Sox since they signed him as a free agent two years ago following exceptional work with the New York Yankees. He recorded 34 saves in 2015 and another 44 this season with an outstanding earned run average of 1.83.

Tonight's appearance is no exception. He gets Baez and Rizzo in order on two pop outs, and then strikes out Bryant on a beautiful curve ball, a total of only 11 pitches thrown that inning.

Adam LaRoche leads off the bottom of the ninth against Hammel and lines a hard drive down the right field line, but it falls outside the white line and is foul. He grounds out on the next pitch and Hammel strikes out the next two batters. Now it's onward to extra innings with some wonderment over who will pitch for the Sox.

The mystery is quickly answered when Robertson comes back out of the dugout toward the hill. There are, however, two pitchers throwing in the bullpen.

"You'll have your relief ace one more inning, if even that. Then who? We've got Hammel, our number four pitcher, and he's just getting started," Katie turns to boast to her husband Tom and Jeff. "Joe Maddon is a super brain when it comes to juggling, or not juggling, his pitchers. I'll take his judgment every time over Robin-hood."

She is quickly proven to be right.

Robertson's second pitch of the inning to Soler is lined into right center field and only an incredible jump on the ball by Eaton prevents it from turning into extra bases. Starlin Castro is next and immediately goes into a bunting stance, but misses the first pitch.

He takes two balls, and then on the fourth pitch hits a hard ground ball up the middle that appears headed for center field.

But Sox shortstop Ramirez dives, stabs the ball and while on his back finds enough energy to shuffle the ball to second baseman Sanchez for a force play and the first out of the inning.

"Incredible play, way to go Alexei," Tom jumps up and yells. "Imagine, we almost traded him last year. Thank God we didn't, although he hasn't hit as well as he used to."

Montero is next and on the third pitch hits a ground ball to Sanchez, who quickly turns it into a second to shortstop to first double play and out of the inning.

Outfielder Trayce Thompson bats for Sanchez to start the bottom of the 10th. He's a young outfielder from Los Angeles, who was a top White Sox top draft pick in 2009 and played well in the minor leagues, like so many other good looking prospects. Thompson possesses great speed and is an exciting center-fielder who can also hit, often with power.

He earned a trip to the major league team in August, 2015 after hitting .287 with six home runs during the first half of the season at Charlotte, the team's Triple A club.

With the Sox, he did exceptionally well after being brought up, hitting an excellent .295 with five home runs and distinguishing himself as a very good outfielder. This year he's batting a respectable .289, primarily as a spot starter and frequent defensive replacement with 10 long balls.

Big-time sports is nothing new to Trayce. His father, Mychal, was a standout member of the Los Angeles Lakers for many years and his older brother, Klay, is a great shooting guard with the Golden State Warriors and played a significant role in their 2015 NBA championship.

"I wish Ventura would have used him more as a starter. He's got a good eye and a fair amount of pop in his bat besides being a really good outfielder," Tom says, leaning toward Jeff.

"You never know what might happen with a young player like this making his first appearance in the World Series," chimes in Jeff. "My great-grandfather told me plenty of great stories over the years about players his great-grandfather wrote about as a sports journalist in the early to mid-1900s."

Just as those words come out of Jeff's mouth, Thompson connects. He hits a long blast into left center field off Hammel that drives Fowler back to the wall. He leaps and the ball deflects off the top of his fielding glove and over the fence for a game winning home run. The White Sox capture game one of the 2016 World Series 3-2 in ten innings.

Bedlam breaks loose at U.S. Cellular Field. Thompson rounds the bases with a gigantic grin on his face and is mobbed by his teammates at home plate.

He motions to his family in the stands who are also in a big-time cheering mode. "I can't believe this," says Mychal Thompson, "an NBA title for one son and a year later a game winning World Series home run for another and hopefully a championship here also."

It's very reminiscent of the game-winning home run by Scott Podsednik in the bottom of the 9th inning to give the White Sox a 7-6 win over the Houston Astros in game 2 of the 2005 World Series. The Sox went on to sweep the series.

White Sox fans are delirious, jumping up and down, while Cubs fans are sad, but reflective and confident their super young team will bounce back. "It's only one game and it takes four to win the title," a somber Cubs fan yells toward the Sox festivities.

Chapter 8 – Game 2 – October 10, 1906 World Series

"A One-Hit Wonder"

"So, here we are again, back at U.S. Cellular Field. It's the first time a World Series has ever been played in the same ballpark three straight days, or nights in this case, in a row," Jeff O'Fallon tells Mr. and Mrs. Tom Buchanan two hours before the start of game 2 between the White Sox and Cubs.

"When the teams last played for the championship in 1906, the Sox also won the first game, that time in just one day without a suspended game that had to be finished two days later," O'Fallon, whose great-great-great grandfather was a sportswriter then, explains. "That time the game was never in doubt."

"Because the teams switched between their home ballparks for every game, this contest was played at South Side Park, also known as the 39th Street Grounds, then the White Sox home field.

"The park was on the north side of 39th Street, now known as Pershing Road, between South Wentworth and South Princeton Avenues.

"It was originally the playing field of the Chicago Wanderers cricket team and used during the 1893 World's Fair, also known as the Columbian Exposition. White Sox owner Charles Comiskey built a wooden grandstand on the site, after which it became the White Sox home field until 1910. That's when the team moved from that location, known as a major fire hazard and tinder box, to the new steel and concrete Comiskey Park just four blocks away.

"South Side Park eventually became the home of the Negro League team, the Chicago American Giants. They played there until 1940 when a fierce Christmas Day fire very quickly destroyed the facility.

"The Giants then played at Comiskey Park until the team disbanded in 1950, three years after baseball became integrated."(56)

"Nearly 13-thousand fans crammed into the ball yard for Game 2. The Cubs sent their second-best pitcher after "Three Finger" Brown in Ed Reulbach, who had a brilliant 19-4 record that season, to the mound. The White Sox countered with Doc White, who led the American League with a 1.52 earned run average and an impressive 18-6 record.

"But White wasn't feeling well that day. He had a bad cold and didn't like pitching in the chilly weather. By the end of the third inning, the Cubs led 4-0, with all of those runs being unearned as the Sox made three errors.

"The Cubs three great and most memorable field players, shortstop Joe Tinker, second baseman Johnny Evers and slugging first baseman Frank Chance ran all over the bases that day, scoring and hitting at will.

"Reulbach pitched the first of six one-hit games in World Series history. The only White Sox hit in the game came in the seventh inning off the bat of first baseman Jiggs Donahue.

"From what I understand about that game, the Sox never had a chance. Reulbach couldn't be touched and the Sox not only gave away runs with careless errors but also weren't thinking at all on the field or at bat and were swinging at pitches way out of the strike zone," O'Fallon adds.

"The next World Series one-hitter didn't come until 39 years later and coincidentally involved another Cubs pitcher. This time Claude Passeau gave up a second-inning single to the Detroit Tigers Rudy York in the 1945 World Series. The Cubs also won that game, 3-0.

"There were some other very interesting pitchers in that 1906 series," he further explains. For the Cubs, Reulbach, that game's winning pitcher, was considered by *Baseball Magazine* one of the greatest pitchers ever in the National League besides being a real gentleman. When pitching, he used "shadowing" or hiding the ball in his windup which made it much more difficult to hit, as well as a very high leg kick like Juan Marichal.

"He was also very intelligent having attended the University of Notre Dame before transferring his senior year to the University of Vermont Medical School to be closer to his future wife. He went directly from Vermont to the Cubs. He had two winning streaks of more than 14 games in his career. Teammate Johnny Evers considered him a "brain," saying that he was always five years ahead of his time in baseball thought," Jeff finishes. (57)

"That's very impressive and hurrah for the Cubs for signing him," says Katie.

"Even I, as a Sox fan, have to second that. It's not what you think of when you discuss old time players," agrees Tom.

"Now, the White Sox weren't short of intelligent players. Frank Owen, the capable right-handed pitcher for the South Siders, had a medical degree and had attended Michigan Agricultural College, now Michigan State University.

"During the Spanish-American War, he served with his father in the Hospital Corps and worked as a physician during the off-season. He was discovered by Clark Griffith while he was scouting "Three Finger" Brown. When the Sox couldn't sign Brown, they opted for Owen.

"In 1905, he became the first major league pitcher to throw two complete game victories on the same day. My grandfather told me that his grandfather who covered the game said it was an incredible feat," (58) says Jeff.

"Your stories really make the 1906 series come to life. Thanks so much for sharing it with us. Enjoy the rest of your evening and we'll see you tomorrow," Tom chimes in.

Chapter 9 – Game 2 – October 24, 2016 World Series

The third day of World Series baseball, but only the second game, matches left-handers Jon Lester of the Cubs and Carlos Rodon of the White Sox.

Lester has had a brilliant career, primarily with the Boston Red Sox, as well as Oakland and now the Cubs.

He is also a cancer survivor. In August of 2006, he was diagnosed with enlarged lymph nodes and tested for a variety of ailments, including forms of cancer. Doctors at Massachusetts General Hospital confirmed that Lester had a treatable form of anaplastic large cell lymphoma. By December of that year, *ESPN.com* reported that Lester's latest CT scan showed no signs of the disease, which appeared to be in remission. (59)

He returned to action the following season and was a key part of the Red Sox World Series titles over Colorado in 2007 and St. Louis in 2013.

White Sox starter Rodon completed his second full season with the team by posting 17 wins with a 2.83 earned run average (ERA).

The Cubs, still feeling the sting of Trayce Thompson's game-winning home run the previous night, jump on Rodon from the start.

Leadoff man Fowler lashes a double down the right-field line. Then on the third pitch he sees, Bryant hits another moon shot, high and very far, only unlike the previous time, this one is a fair ball, 485 feet away and a 2-0 Cubs lead before many fans even get to their seats. This home run is comparable to the gigantic blasts he hit the previous May and August at Wrigley Field against Washington and Arizona.

"Incredible. Way to go, Kris." Katie shouts. "This is our game and that's a great start."

She next turns to her husband Tom and softly says, "With that kind of excitement, I might end up having this baby a lot sooner than we think."

Rodon shakes his head as he watches Bryant trot around the bases. The Sox pitcher has been very good throughout this season with his 17 wins, but has consistently been scored upon in the first inning of many games.

Big things have been expected from Bryant in the majors from the minute he signed with the Cubs. He's been described as the best player ever at the University of San Diego (USD), which has had a solid baseball program for years.

Among the standouts who played at USD is John Wathan, holder of the record for most stolen bases in a season by a catcher in major league history. That occurred in 1982 when he swiped 36 as a member of the Kansas City Royals.

Longtime baseball coach Rich Hill made it very clear the Cubs were getting a special player and told the school's *Inside USD Magazine*, "He was a program changer for us. He worked extremely hard at his craft and he wants to be the best. Combined with his character and everything else, he was absolutely special. He was a once-in-a-career type of player. We look forward to watching him for many years to come." (60)

Equally as excited about Bryant's potential is Jay Johnson, a former assistant at USD, who now is the head baseball coach at the University of Nevada. "I'm proud of Kris," he said. "His decision to come to USD took the program to another level. Getting the opportunity to coach him day in, day out was a great privilege. I'm very excited to watch his career grow. Over time Cubs fans will really develop an appreciation for how he plays the game." (61)

Cubs fans are loving both Bryant and Lester this night of the second game of the 2016 World Series.

Lester holds the White Sox scoreless through four innings with only a single by Thompson, who is in the starting lineup tonight after his dramatic home run to win game one.

Rodon is equally as tough since Bryant's blast. He's now retired 10 batters in a row, five of them strikeouts.

The Sox begin to make some noise in the bottom of the fifth. Catcher Vlessen singles to open the inning. Thompson follows with a beautiful bunt which squiggles past Lester. It's intended to be a sacrifice, but is so perfectly placed it goes for another hit.

That brings up Eaton who everyone is expecting to also lay down a sacrifice bunt to move the base runners. He tries that twice without success as Lester throws him sinker balls down and in. After two balls, Eaton can only hit a soft popup to Castro for the first out. Then Cabrera pulls a hard ground ball to Rizzo, which he quickly converts into a first to shortstop to first double play. So much for that rally!

The game remains 2-0 into the top of the seventh when the Cubs take their turn to get some base runners. Castro singles on a ground ball up the middle, then steals second on the first pitch to Baez. He flies out, but catcher Montero hits a soft flair over the third baseman's head and by the time Ramirez gets to the ball in short left field, Castro is crossing the plate to make the score 3-0.

It's seventh inning stretch time for White Sox fans. Once again Chicago's own Buckinghams get the crowd fired up with a rousing version of "Take Me Out to the Ballgame."

Lester easily retires the first two batters in the inning and is still sailing along with just 84 pitches thrown. Designated hitter Adam LaRoche next belts a long drive to right field that Soler nearly runs down, but it hits off his glove and even the slow-footed batter has no problems legging out a triple.

Avisail Garcia, the right-fielder, is next and reaches over the outside corner to punch a low curve ball at his knees for a single into center field, scoring LaRoche, to make it a 3-1 ballgame.

"Get Lester out of there. He's getting tired and can't control his pitches anymore," Katie yells at the top of her lungs. A look toward the Cubs bullpen shows Pedro Strop, the team's regular set-up pitcher, hastily warming up.

Maddon picks up the vibe and slowly strolls out of the dugout toward the mound where he is joined by all the infielders. He chats for a minute or two with his standout pitcher and then points to the bullpen to send in Strop.

Shortstop Ramirez is the next White Sox batter. He can be very tough in situations like this, but also has the ability to make himself look bad by taking wild swings and going after pitches way out of the strike zone.

Strop's first pitch is a perfect strike, which Ramirez takes and watches go into the catcher's glove. After a ball, the shortstop sees a pitch he likes from the moment it leaves the pitcher's hand. He swings and hits the ball a long distance, but foul down the left field line. That's his one good pitch to hit, so it seems, as he strikes out on the next offering without even coming close.

Daniel Webb enters the game for Rodon in the top of the eighth and starts off with a walk to Cubs shortstop Russell, the number nine hitter.

. Webb has been a promising pitcher for three seasons now with only marginal success. He looks like a potential star reliever at times, getting batters out with seeming ease. On other occasions though, it's a big struggle for him to get the ball over the plate and his control is a big bugaboo.

"Come on Webb. Concentrate out there on the mound. Throw strikes," Buchanan angrily yells at the Sox reliever. "Don't give them baserunners."

Fowler is up next and immediately goes into a bunting stance, but Webb's first two pitches are wide. That brings a big moan of discontent with the predominantly large number of White Sox fans.

The third pitch is over for a strike, bringing a Bronx, sarcastic, cheer. Then on the fourth pitch, Maddon takes off the bunt sign and Fowler lashes a single into left field. Two on with no one out and up steps Mr. Power Plus, one of many nicknames Bryant has acquired as a member of the Cubs.

He's bunted on a few occasions this season, but that's not his role. Everyone knows he's a long ball hitter and RBI man.

White Sox pitching coach Don Cooper calls time and strolls to the mound. He appears to give Webb a tongue-lashing, then pats him on the behind and shouts words of encouragement.

"Oh boy, I fear the worst here. This guy Webb has so much potential, but just can't consistently get the job done," O'Fallon yells to the Buchanans over the crowd noise.

Bryant appears ready to crush a pitch as the crowd gets very, very loud. The first one comes in at the letters on his uniform and is called a ball. Then he hits a foul ball down the right field line. Webb proceeds to throw two more balls that aren't even close. With a 3-1 count in his favor, Bryant is now ready for the kill and the next pitch indeed is very much to his liking.

He hits a bullet-like ground ball right to third baseman Tyler Saladino, who is standing almost directly on the bag. The crowd is shell-shocked. The ball couldn't have been hit harder and looks like a sure hit. Within a matter of a heartbeat, it suddenly now looks like a rare third to second to first triple play!

Not quite, Bryant barely beats the toss from second to first by less than a second. Webb and the rest of the Sox team are truly pumped up and he proceeds to strike out Rizzo on three pitches.

Strop is back out on the mound for the Cubs in the bottom of the eighth and has little trouble quickly getting out Saladino, Vlessen and pinch hitter Bobby Holmes, the 7, 8 and 9 batters for the White Sox.

The Cubs also go out in order in the top of the ninth and in from the bullpen comes their closer, Hector Rondon. He's the outstanding Venezuelan flamethrower, who has 48 saves during the regular season.

He gets Eaton and Cabrera for the first two outs. Abreu lashes a line drive down the left field line on the first pitch, then plays a cat and mouse game with Rondon, fouling off pitch after pitch until the 13th toss of the at bat. He sends that one soaring deep to right center. Fowler gives chase but can only watch as the ball travels far into the bleachers to cut the Cubs lead to 3-2.

LaRoche is next and he hits a long foul ball into the right field corner on the first pitch, which sends a scare into the hearts of Cubs fans. But their concern is short-lived as he grounds out to Russell to end the game.

The series is tied at a game apiece, a 3-2 win for each team. North side fans sing their team's song, "Go Cubs Go," loudly as they exit U.S. Cellular Field. From here the action resumes tomorrow at Wrigley Field, the first World Series game played in the newly renovated and remodeled park at Addison and Clark since 1945, 71 years ago!

Chapter 10 – Game 3 – October 11, 1906

Here Comes "Big Ed"

It was back to the Cubs' West Side Park for game three of the 1906 all Chicago World Series.

"This time the Sox brought out their rising young star, 'Big Ed' Walsh, who had a legendary career that was unfortunately cut short by injuries," says Jeff O'Fallon.

"On this weather plagued, chilly afternoon, the announced crowd was only 13,667 and they saw a masterpiece. While the Cubs Reulbach threw a one-hitter the previous day, Walsh gave up just two hits in hurling a 3-0 shutout win with 12 strikeouts. He also played a role in the scoring.

"Jack Pfiester pitched well for the Cubs and only gave up four hits as the White Sox scored all their runs in the sixth inning.

"After a leadoff single, Walsh managed to earn a walk (no designated hitters then) and Pfiester was so flustered he next hit leadoff batter Ed "Noodles" Hahn in the face, breaking his nose. Bases loaded with none out. The next two batters hit easy pop-up outs, but Pfiester then gave up a bases clearing triple down the left field line. All three runs scored and Walsh took over from there, not allowing any more base runners. It gave the South Siders a 2-1 lead in the series.

"From everything I ever heard about Walsh, via my family connections, he was a total workhorse who always wanted the ball," O'Fallon explains further. "He had a secret weapon, the spitball, which a lot of guys threw then. It wasn't outlawed until 1920, after Big Ed had retired. Of course there have been many pitchers over the years who have thrown it despite the ban, most notably Hall of Famer Gaylord Perry. He won 314 games during a 21-year career from 1962 to 1983 with eight different teams and got away with it."

"A spitball basically is an illegal pitch in which the ball has been altered by the application of saliva, petroleum jelly or some other foreign substance. This technique alters the wind resistance and weight on one side of the ball, causing it to move in an atypical manner. It may also cause the ball to "slip" out of the pitcher's fingers without the usual spin that accompanies a pitch. In this sense, a spitball can be thought of as a fastball with knuckleball action.

Hall of Fame player Sam Crawford is quoted in Lawrence Ritter's book, *"The Glory of Their Times,"* "Walsh was a great big, strong, good looking fellow. I think his spitball disintegrated on the way to the plate, and the catcher put it back together again. I swear, when it went past the plate, only the spit went by."

'Walsh's first full season with the White Sox came in 1906, when he won 17 games, with an earned run average (ERA) of 1.88 along with 171 strikeouts.

'He had worked in the Luzerne County, Pennsylvania coal mines when he was still in school, but eventually started his baseball career in 1902 at the age of 21. The White Sox brought him to the major league team two years later and he soon became a big star.

'Between 1906 and 1912, Walsh was totally dominant. He averaged 24 wins each year, 220 strikeouts and posted an ERA below 2.00 five different times He also led the league in saves five times during that span. His best individual season came in 1908 when he posted an almost unfathomable 40 wins with 15 losses, 269 strikeouts, 6 saves and a remarkable 1.42 ERA.

"In fact, his career ERA of 1.82 is the lowest in major league history. It's not considered an official statistic, however, because ERA numbers weren't legitimately kept prior to 1913. Walsh's arm eventually tuckered out and his remarkable career was over by 1916."

He later recalled in a story in the *Chicago Herald-American* newspaper, "I could feel the muscles grind and wrench during the games, and it seemed my arm might leap out of my socket when I threw the ball. Unfortunately, my arm would keep me awake until morning with a pain I'd never felt before."

"He finished with 195 career wins, 126 losses and 1,736 strikeouts and was inducted into baseball's Hall of Fame in 1946. He died in 1959, another year in which the White Sox won the American League pennant and made the World Series, at the age of 78." (62)

"Since the White Sox won game three, let's begin by talking about one of their star players in the 1906 Series. Pat Dougherty didn't even join the team until the middle of July. He had left the New York

Highlanders over a contract dispute and played for an "outlaw" team until Fielder Jones found him. Dougherty and Jones attended the same high school, but not at the same time. In fact, Jones helped Dougherty get a job in the Eastern League before he got to the majors in 1904," explains O'Fallon.

"The family story as passed down to me was that Dougherty was a very good outfielder and helped defensively with his excellent range. The Highlanders protested the signing and appealed to American League President Ban Johnson who ruled for the Sox, although giving Dougherty a 10-game suspension for playing on the unofficial team after leaving New York," O'Fallon adds.

"However much he helped the White Sox win the pennant, he did not play well in the World Series. His importance to the team that year cannot be overlooked, because of his contribution getting them to the championship games," Jeff says as he concludes the story of Dougherty. (63)

Tom says, "I had never even heard of Patrick Dougherty let alone know of how he solidified the outfield and helped get the Sox to the World Series.

Your family is a fountain of information about the early days of baseball."

"Thanks for the kind words, Tom. Our Cubs player today is Jack Pfiester who pitched game three. He had a great game, despite losing. Remember, the score was 3-0."

"That should be interesting. Did he have the same type of background as the players you told us about yesterday?" Katie asks.

"No, Katie, not quite. No doctors or lawyers today. Pfiester pitched in the majors for over eight seasons, ending with an excellent 2.02 ERA. He's best remembered for the seven shutouts and 15-5 record against the New York Giants.

"He was born John Hagenbush and changed his last name unofficially to Pfiester when his parents died and his aunt and uncle, whose last name was Pfiester, raised him. He came up with the Pirates in 1902, but was sent down to Omaha after having a few bad seasons in Pittsburgh. The Cubs bought his contract in 1906. In May of that year, he struck out 17 batters in 15 innings, a record that stood until Warren Spahn broke it in 1952.

"His record in 1906, as a rookie, included a 1.51 ERA, fewest hits per game, 153 strikeouts and 20 wins which made him a huge factor in the Cubs incredible season.   In his game three loss, he only allowed 4 hits by the White Sox and struck out 9. He pitched in relief in game 5 without much success. You'll hear more about him when I tell you about game five," Jeff adds.

"He was around for the Cubs 1907 and 1908 World Series championships. He won game 2 in 1907 giving up three hits in a 3-1 Cubs victory over Detroit," he continues.

"And he also was the winning pitcher in the famous "Merkle's Boner" game against the New York Giants. It was a one-game playoff after the teams tied for the 1908 National League pennant. That's when the Giants' Fred Merkle failed to touch second base in a key situation. Furthermore, it turns out that Pfiester pitched the entire game with a dislocated arm. There wasn't any such thing as Tommy John surgery then!" (64)

"Let's meet under the big Wrigley Field sign on Addison Street tomorrow before the game. I can't wait to hear more about 1906. Will you also tell us something about your great-great-great grandfather and his life?" asks Katie.

Chapter 11 – Game 3 – October 25, 2016 World Series

The Cubs are finally playing at home, in the first World Series contest at Wrigley Field since October, 1945.

Today it's a battle of young right-handers, who are both from California and were big stars in college, Kyle Hendricks for the Cubs and Erik Johnson for the White Sox.

Hendricks was raised in Newport Beach and received his degree in economics from Dartmouth College in the Ivy League. It's no surprise that his nickname is "The Professor." He was named the Cubs Minor League Pitcher of the Year in 2013.

Johnson grew up in Mountain View. He was a pitching standout at the Pac 12's University of California. He floundered somewhat in the Sox organization until 2015 when he was named the International League's Pitcher of the Year with Charlotte when he won 11 games..

"This is incredible to see a World Series game here at Wrigley Field. My great-great-great grandfather is almost turning over in his grave, he's so excited. He covered the last White Sox-Cubs World Series in 1906. What a thrill this would be for him to see, as well as other members of my fanatical baseball family," Jeff O'Fallon says to Katie and Tom.

The pre-game festivities and ceremonies are huge with people milling about everywhere on Addison, Sheffield, Waveland and Clark as early as three hours before the first pitch. Seats for this historic game reportedly have been selling for up to $10,000 each through Stub Hub and elsewhere, including even on the street.

Once it's time to "play ball," virtually everyone among the 40,000 fans is in a frenzy of being part of a history making event at the venerable ballpark.

And when Hendricks retires the Sox in order in the top of the first on just 11 pitches, Cubs fans already are sensing a big day for the team that hasn't won a World Series in more than a century.

In the bottom of the first, Johnson quickly displays his penchant for sometimes being inconsistent. He walks Fowler on five pitches and also gets behind Schwarber before giving up a single. Rizzo is next and after faking a bunt on the first pitch, he hits a hard line drive to center fielder Eaton, who gets a good jump and makes a sliding, diving catch.

Third baseman Bryant, batting cleanup, doesn't waste any time, hitting the first pitch over the third base bag into the left field corner for a double, scoring Fowler and sending Schwarber to third with Bryant coasting into second.

Johnson is visited by manager Ventura to talk over the situation. He obviously realizes how critical it is for him to keep the damage to a minimum and hopefully prevent anyone else from touching home plate.

It doesn't seem likely when he throws three straight balls to Soler, but then gets him to foul off a pitch, swing through another in the dirt and take a called third strike that has him make a disparaging comment to home plate umpire Gabriel Ramirez. Maddon is livid and begins to scream from the dugout at the man behind the plate, which earns him a quick ejection.

Maddon rushes out of the dugout to give Ramirez a piece of his mind as the crowd cheers wildly. Meantime, Johnson is throwing a few warmup pitches to stay ready. When catcher Montero weakly pops out to Abreu in foul territory, the first inning is over with the Cubs ahead 1-0.

"Too bad the Cubs couldn't get that second run across. It could come back to bite them later," O'Fallon shouts out.

"I can't believe that Soler couldn't just make contact to hit a sac fly or even a ground ball. The White Sox infield was playing back and willing to concede that run," Katie adds.

"We'll see how it plays out, honey. I doubt if Johnson is going to proceed from here without giving up another run. It's up to the Sox now to get something started against Hendricks and keep pounding away," Tom replies to his wife.

Avisail Garcia must have heard what Buchanan said. He goes after the third pitch he sees and lashes a hard line drive into the left center field gap. It's a certain double, but Garcia defies a cardinal rule of baseball, not to make the first or last out of an inning at third base. He is easily thrown out by Fowler in center field to relay man Castro to Bryant at third.

Cub fans love it and burst into a cacophony of rousing cheers. Two soft ground ball outs follow and the White Sox trail 1-0 after two innings.

By the end of the fifth, it has totally become a pitcher's duel. Each team has just three hits as the Cubs hold onto their scant lead. Hendricks and Johnson are dominant, appearing to be unhittable while striking out batters with great efficiency.

Into the sixth, it's catcher Vlessen who hits the first offering from Hendricks 420 feet on a line into the center field bleachers to tie the game 1-1. As he rounds the bases, the ball he hit or a replica of it, sails back on the field and nearly beans center fielder Fowler. He nonchalantly tosses it back into the infield.

"What kind of an idiot, in a game with such historic significance, would throw a homerun ball back onto the field? Maybe it's a ball he just brought here today," Buchanan speculates. "Whatever the case, it's a stupid, bush league thing to do. That ball is definitely a keepsake, no matter who hit it."

Katie, a Cubs fan from the day she was born, quickly turns toward the father of her soon to be born child, "Listen to Mister "Right Way" here. Let a good Cubs fan have some fun, will you? We haven't had many chances to let loose with total excitement and chaos for our team!"

Tom casually looks the other way toward Jeff and rolls his eyes, then slowly turns toward Katie, and puts his finger over his lips. He just wants her to shut the f*** up when it comes to her goddamn Wrigley wretches, as he sometimes calls them.

He loves her dearly, always has, but her obsession with that team drives him crazy at times. Of course, now isn't the time to make a scene with her about to give birth.

Both teams are unable to get anything started until the top of the eighth when Ramirez comes up for the White Sox and grounds a ball up the middle past Hendricks for a single. He's then replaced at first by pinch-runner Micah Johnson.

Next up is Abreu. Surely this big power hitter won't be bunting. That's what everyone in the ballpark is assuming. But his gigantic swing connects with just a smidgen of the ball and it slowly dribbles down the third-base line. It stays fair for an infield hit meaning two men on with no one out.

Pitching coach Chris Bosio brings in right handed relief pitcher Strop. The huge crowd breathes a huge gulp of amazement when Garcia, another power hitter, lays down a beautiful bunt which he beats out and the bases are now loaded with no one out. Vlessen walks to bring home Johnson and give the White Sox a 2-1 lead.

After an infield pop-up results in an automatic out, third baseman Tyler Saladino hits what appears to be a certain double-play ball to shortstop Russell. He flips to Castro at second for an apparent force out on Vlessen on a very close play. But his throw to first bounces into Saladino, then off Rizzo.

That sends Abreu and Garcia home, making the score 4-1. Vlessen, not realizing he's been called out at second, races for third base. Meantime, Rizzo gets the ball and fires to second base where Saladino becomes caught in a rundown.

The rundown then prompts the Sox third-base coach to send Vlessen home. Russell now hears teammates yelling "home" as Vlessen rounds third and is eventually tagged out at the plate, thanks to an excellent swipe tag by catcher Montero.

The Cubs now think there are three outs, despite the fact that Vlessen has been called out twice on the same play. The team trots off the field.

That brings Ventura flying out of the White Sox dugout to confront home plate umpire Ramirez and argue that the same man cannot be called out twice among the three outs.

"Wait a minute," Jeff O'Fallon yells to Katie and Tom Buchanan, who are sitting next to him. "That play is virtually identical to what happened in a Cubs-Phillies game on August 3rd of 1906. In that case, the game was already out of hand with the Cubs way ahead, so it didn't affect the overall outcome. My grandfather told me about that game several times based on what his grandfather told him when he covered that game for the *Chicago Gazette*.

"This is a much different situation and I can only imagine what a brouhaha this is going to result in."

The 1906 game had the Cubs' Harry Steinfeldt being called out twice, at both second base and home plate. In those days, there only were two umpires, one at home plate and the other standing behind the pitchers, calling the plays at each base.

There also was no access to television replays back in the early days of baseball since TV broadcasts didn't begin until the 1940s. But equipment was very primitive until the 1960s and replays didn't occur until even later than that.

The umpires, all six of them including two men who patrol the left and right field foul lines besides the home plate and base arbiters, are now gathered around Ramirez trying to sort this out.

Replays on the WOLF network, which is carrying the game worldwide with 15 cameras in place around the ballpark, cannot determine if Vlessen is safe or out at second base. The umpire there, Moe East, called him out with a very weak signal.

In the sky box housing baseball's top brass, Commissioner Rob Manfred huddles with MLB and WOLF executives, trying to figure out the best solution to this chaotic situation the umpires seem to have created for themselves.

"In the 1906 mess, it wasn't decided until after the game was over that the runner was officially ruled out at second. That meant the final score was changed from 8-0 to 7-0. Now over a century later you have basically the same play, along with six umpires and a multitude of high-tech television and electronic tools, and they don't seem to know what to do," O'Fallon adds.

Home plate umpire Ramirez and second base referee East are on the headphones to MLB headquarters in New York reviewing the play at second base.

That's where East made the very lame "out" call, limply and casually lifting his arm up after hesitating at least three to four seconds as Vlessen, slid in, then got up and kept running all the way home, where he was clearly tagged out this time and called "out."

After nearly four minutes of talking with New York, the headphone umpires finally reach a decision. They determine Vlessen is out at second, and is ejected from the game for "showboating" by disregarding East's "out" call and trying to show him up.

"I felt strongly that I was safe, so I just got up from my slide and kept running. Next thing I see is our third base coach waving me home," Vlessen later told the Chicago Defender.

The normally mild-mannered Ventura, who is often criticized for his laid-back California-ish style, goes ballistic. He kicks dirt over home plate, then gets face to face with both Ramirez and East and is obviously kicked out of the game.

The only other time he's displayed such a demonstrative reaction as the team's manager came on an August afternoon in San Francisco in 2014 where a call went against the Sox on a play involving then catcher Tyler Flowers' questionable way of blocking the plate. It cost the team the game.

So, it reverts back to two outs with Saladino on first. But the Sox are now so furious to a man over the way this play has been handled that it's no surprise when second baseman Carlos Sanchez, mostly a "Punch and Judy" singles type hitter, pulverizes the first pitch far into the bleachers for a two-run homer.

That brings the score to 6-1 White Sox. A long pinch-hit home run by the Cubs Robby Ramizotti in the bottom of the ninth makes the final score 6-2.

"I thought the Cubs would have all the momentum in their first World Series home game in 71 years," Tom says to Katie and Jeff as the three get ready to join the masses exiting the ballpark named after the Cubs former owner, William Wrigley, the chewing gum magnate.

"I felt very positive all last night and today that the Cubs would pull ahead in the series," she replies. "These games are so pressure filled I don't know if I can make it through another one without having this baby. My heart is constantly pounding, with almost every pitch. I just hope the Cubs can truly put it all together tomorrow and even up this series at two games each."

Chapter 12 – Game 4 – October 12, 1906 World Series

"Columbus Day Gem"

Finally, decent weather on Columbus Day with sunny skies and temperatures in the 60s as the teams get ready to play game four.

More than 18,000 fans are gathered for a sellout at the White Sox home field, South Side Park on 39th Street (Pershing Road). It's a pitching rematch between the Cubs' Mordecai "Three Finger" Brown and Nick Altrock of the White Sox, who won game one, 2-1.

This time the future Hall of Famer Brown prevailed 1-0 with a brilliant two-hitter. He had a no-hitter for 5 2/3 innings before giving up a hit.

Two members of the Cubs' famed infield trio of Tinkers to Evers to Chance figured prominently in the one run scored, along with Sox right-fielder "Noodles" Hahn.

With his broken nose temporarily repaired by using just tobacco juice and masking tape, Hahn lost Frank Chance's fly ball in the sun for a single to start the seventh inning. Two sacrifice bunts sent him to third base where he scored on a single by Johnny Evers.

The White Sox made an effort to tie the game in the bottom of the ninth on a walk followed by a passed ball to move the runner to second, into scoring position. But Frank Isbell grounded out to douse the threat and end the game.

The series is now tied at two games each. Tightly pitched, close contests have prevailed in three of the first four games.

There is speculation that the White Sox will start "Big Ed" Walsh again tomorrow in game five with just one day of rest! Imagine that 110 years later in 2016?

"So with the series tied 2-2, the suspense continues and it's time to tell you more about some of the men who played in that World Series, just as I promised. I'll hold off telling you about my great-great-great grandfather until later in our time together," Jeff begins.

"Let's start with John "Jiggs" Donahue who began his major league career with the Pittsburgh Pirates in 1901. "The Old Roman" Comiskey bought his contract in 1903 and he played first base for the White Sox for five seasons. Comiskey got him for his fielding ability at first base, not as a hitter.

"Not surprisingly, he led the American League in fielding averages, putouts and assists for a first baseman for 3 years, including 1906. He also still holds the record for most putouts in a year, 1,846 in 1907. But to the surprise of everyone, he tied George Rohe for the highest batting average in the World Series, proving that you can't believe all the statistics in important situations. He had a lifetime .255 average!"

"He also got the White Sox hit to break up Ed Reulbach's no-hitter in game three of the series. Eventually, he was traded from the Sox as his years at first base affected his overall ability. But his life, as well as his career was short. He retired and returned to Chicago to run a bowling alley and died in 1913 after a long illness. A World Series hero who didn't get to enjoy his life for very long," Jeff concludes. (64)

"How tragic for a World Series standout on the 'Hitless Wonders'," Tom says.

"Here's another player who played a major role in the series and also had a sad ending. Harry Steinfeldt had one of the bunts that moved Frank Chance around the bases to eventually score the winning run in game four," begins Jeff.

"While many players go from baseball to entertainment, Harry did it the other way. As a child and young man he toured Texas in a minstrel show, playing baseball on the side. He was signed by Cincinnati in 1898 and played for them several years before being traded to the Cubs in 1906 and having a career year. One Chicago reporter, not my great-great-great grandfather, wrote that the 'addition of these two stars made the Cubs the greatest baseball machine in the country.' By that he was talking about (Jimmy) Sheckard and Steinfeldt."

"After retiring from baseball, he went to work in his father-in-law's bread-pan factory, which he did not enjoy. He tried going back to baseball with no success and died of a cerebral hemorrhage at the age of 37." (66)

"What sad endings to the lives of two men who were so important to their respective teams in 1906. Thanks for telling us their stories. Tom and I didn't know anything about them," Katie responds.

Chapter 13 – Game 4 – October 26, 2016 World Series

Back at Wrigley as the Cubs hope to tie up the series, at two games each, just like the 1906 fall classic played out after four games.

Warming up again for the Cubs is Hammel, who finished the continuation of game one and was victimized by Thompson's dramatic game-winning home run.

Left-hander Jose Quintana takes the mound for the White Sox. He's been a mainstay of the team's pitching rotation the past few years, yet is perhaps best known for his uncanny knack of exiting games with a "no decision." He also has a penchant for sometimes falling behind batters in tight situations, resulting in being forced to deliver a "fat pitch" that can be sent a long distance.

Quintana set the American League record in the "no decision" category in 2013 with 17 of them. That fell three short of Bert Blyleven's major league record of 20 in 1979 with the world-champion Pittsburgh Pirates.

Tonight he's already in trouble in the bottom of the first. Rizzo and Bryant each double, giving the Cubs one run and when Castro's belt reaches the seats in left field, it's already 3-0 before many fans have settled into their seats.

"This Quintana is just too much. Many games he looks great, almost unhittable, until about the sixth or seventh inning, then gets in trouble and winds up losing a lead or lets the other team tie the game. That's why he has so many games with neither a win nor a loss," Buchanan angrily says. "I actually wished they had traded him after last season. Tonight he's already in big trouble!"

The trouble continues when left fielder Chris Coghlan triples into the right field corner, then Montero bloops a single down the left field line. That makes it 4-0 with only one out in the inning.

Katie is in ecstasy, cheering loudly and getting the large crowd, which is mostly made up of Cubs fans at Wrigley Field, to join in.

"Looks like we're headed to a three-game series after we tie it up at two wins for each team. Way to hit the ball, Cubbies, whoo! Don't let up for a second. This is our game," Katie blares out.

Quintana finally settles down and holds the Cubs in check through the next three innings, into the fifth.

In the meantime, Hammel has everything working right and strikes out seven batters through four innings. He also induces many soft ground-ball outs while only giving up two harmless singles.

Finally, the White Sox show some sign of life in the top of the fifth. Thompson again takes a liking to one of Hammel's pitches and leads off the inning with a triple that skips past Fowler to the ivy-covered center field wall. He scores on a sacrifice fly, then with two out, Abreu launches a long blast to left that flies past the video board and shatters a window in the apartment building on the other side of Waveland.

Hammel shrugs his shoulders and strikes out Garcia to end the inning.

The Cubs decide to play some long ball of their own in the bottom of the fifth. With two out, Fowler, Rizzo and Bryant go back to back to back, three long record-breaking home runs in a row to push the score up to 8-2. It is the only time in World Series history that a team has hit three consecutive home runs.

Quintana departs the game shell-shocked. The White Sox appear to be so beaten down, one wonders if they'll ever recover.

Even though they score three more runs, mostly on insignificant hits off Hammel and two relievers, the game is never in doubt after the homer barrage. The Cubs seem to pack up their bats in a steamer trunk for the rest of the night, to preserve them for the next game.

Wrigleyville is abuzz with overzealous Cubs fans yelling, screaming and practically declaring themselves the World Series champions. Katie is beside herself.

"If I have a boy, can we name him Homer to commemorate this incredible night? So many home runs by my wonderful, beloved Cubs!" Katie turns to Tom and asks.

"Hell no," he quickly snaps back to her. "The Cubs kicked our asses here, no doubt about that, but they only won tonight's game and we still have the home field advantage with Chris Sale starting the next game. Just relax and enjoy this historic series. I know I will."

"Take it easy, you two. There's still a lot of baseball to be played," Jeff turns toward both of them while stating the obvious. "I just hope you'll both be around to enjoy all the games in person. That baby must be getting very anxious to join the real world!"

Chapter 14 – Game 5 – October 13, 1906 World Series

Who said baseball fans in the early 1900s didn't have any imagination or creativity?

Back home in West Side Park for game five, two die hard Cubs supporters showed up with snarling young bear cubs and paraded around the ballpark with them. Somehow they managed to get their four-legged friends inside and went immediately to the White Sox bench to show them off.

They next proceeded to let the players pet them and examine their incisors close up.

The White Sox did the rest of the biting on that day and won the contest 8-6.

"That must have been pretty bizarre," Jeff says as he and the Buchanans await the start of the pivotal fifth game of the 2016 World Series. It's tied up at two games each, just like the 1906 series between the White Sox and Cubs.

"But this game, in a series that had been owned by standout pitching, was a slam-bam, wild affair. It featured 18 hits, 10 walks, six errors by the Sox, two hit batsmen, three wild pitches and a steal of home," he adds.

"As had been rumored "Big Ed" Walsh returned to the mound for the White Sox with just one day of rest.

"Imagine any starter coming back to pitch with just one day of rest during this current modern era in baseball," Jeff continues. "It wouldn't happen in a million years."

"But it did and neither Walsh nor Cubs hurler Ed Reulbach, their starter in game two, was very effective. The result was the record paid crowd of 23,257 saw ugly baseball aplenty.

"After the Sox scored a run in the first, the Cubs came back with three unearned runs in the bottom half. Two crossed the plate after a wild throw by second baseman Frank Isbell and another scored when first baseman Jiggs Donahue dropped a throw.

"My great-great-great grandfather, along with just about every other sportswriter and fan in attendance, assumed with a 3-1 lead on their home field, the Cubs would coast home from there against the 'hitless wonder' White Sox," he adds.

"But Walsh, who was just coming into his own as an outstanding pitcher, would have no part of it. He mowed down the Cubs in order in the second and third innings.

"The Sox tied the game 3-3 in the top of the third. Isbell made amends for his throwing error with a double, followed by a single by George Davis, another hit then a true White Sox specialty, a double steal, to even the score. That sent Reulbach to a quick exit and brought on Jack Pfiester, who had opposed Walsh in the third game of the series.

"He was belted around in the fourth for four runs. Isbell and Davis again ignited the rally with back to back doubles, followed by an out, then another two-bagger, this time off the bat of Donahue. Two more hits came and very quickly the Sox had four runs and a 7-3 lead.

"According to what I've heard and read about it, people were amazed the "hitless wonders" put on such a show of hitting. Isbell wound up with four doubles in the game, the only time that's ever been accomplished in a World Series contest," Jeff explains.

"In fact, only 22 players have ever done that in a regular season game. The most recent came in 2006 by former outfielder Matt Murton of the Cubs. Two years earlier, in 2004, the same Adam LaRoche now playing for the Sox hit four doubles in a game when he was a member of the Atlanta Braves.

"Two players have actually accomplished this unusual feat twice in their careers. White Sox outfielder Albert Belle's four-double double happened over a three week span in 1999 as a member of the Baltimore Orioles. And Gavvy Cravath, one of the few long ball hitters during the so-called "dead ball" era prior to Babe Ruth's arrival, accomplished the milestone in both 1915 and 1919 with the Philadelphia Phillies. (67)

"The native of the San Diego County city of Escondido led the major leagues in home runs six times during his career, but never hit more than 24 in a single season.

"The Cubs pecked away with a run in the fourth and two more in the sixth, but it was a White Sox day as they held on for an 8-6 win and a 3-2 lead overall. "Big Ed" Walsh made it through six innings on the mound before handing the ball over to Doc White.

"He proceeded to throw three scoreless innings for the first-ever unofficial recorded save in major league history. Saves did not become an official statistic until decades later, in 1969," Jeff explains.

Most importantly, the White Sox were now within one game of winning a World Series in which the majority of so-called "experts" said they didn't have a "snowball's chance in hell" of a hope. How could these hitless wonders ever have a prayer of beating the Cubs with their 116 wins during the regular season?

Statistically, according to the *Associated Press*, the team that takes a 3-2 lead in the seven-game World Series, has a 71 per cent chance of becoming the champion. That's based on having two chances to capture the clinching win. Would the White Sox accomplish that task the next day when they returned home to their beloved South Side Park?

"Let me tell you something about Frank Isbell who hit the four doubles in that game. Isbell was a fixture as a utility player with the White Sox for almost a decade. Although people remember him as the second baseman in 1906, he was actually one of the few players to play all nine positions during his major league career," adds Jeff.

"He was playing baseball with the St. Paul ball club founded by Comiskey, but left for a few seasons to play for the North side team. When the "Old Roman" moved his team to Chicago, Isbell rejoined his old boss. As a player, he was proud of his ability to play more than a few positions. He claimed that when you're jack-of-all trades, you must always be ready to hit, run or field because you'll surely be called on to do that.'"

"To show you the kind of person he was, consider this story. At one point in time early in his career, he was taking tickets at a game in St. Louis when the grandstand caught on fire. He also noticed a house across the street was burning and watched the family flee. He saw they had left a baby behind. Isbell rushed across the street and rescued the infant."

"1906 was one his best years with a .279 average and .352 slugging percentage. He turned it on in games 5 and 6 of the World Series with the doubles in game 5 and more hits, which you'll hear about next time, in game 6. His had a .308 series average and his record for the most hits in two consecutive series games and most extra base hits in a game has not been topped up to this point. That's saying a lot about what an amazing achievement these records are."

"After he retired, he became a minor league manager and later president of the minor league team in Wichita, Kansas. He also served as a scout for the White Sox and other teams and is credited with developing White Sox Hall of Fame pitcher Urban "Red" Faber," O'Fallon concludes. (68)

"Jeff, you're a fountain of information. Where did you learn about all these old-time players?" asks Tom.

"Most of this is information and stories my great-great-great grandfather told my great-grandfather and they've been passed down by my grandfather and father. It's all a wonderful legacy we're very proud of and love to share with others," says Jeff.

"Ah, but we're not done yet. We can't skip the Cubs player for Katie! This North Sider is considered by sportswriter Joe Reichler to be the Cubs All-Time best left fielder... Jimmy Sheckard, a left-handed slugger who became a leadoff hitter and a master of getting on base for the Cubs."

"My grandfather told me that his great-grandfather said he was in a class by himself in his fielding ability.

Johnny Evers claimed that he was one of the brightest ballplayers he ever knew and that he was much more important to the team in 1906 than anyone outside the clubhouse was aware of. His feeling was Sheckard never received the recognition he deserved for his contributions to the team."

"Part of the reason for that was he was sometimes very inconsistent. So when he was good, he was very good, but at other times not dependable. That is what the family story has said about him."

"Sheckard joined the Cubs from Brooklyn in 1906 and along with Steinfeldt made a huge impact on the club. Jimmy became a team leader and loved to annoy the opposition. He claimed before the World Series began that he would hit .400 against the South Siders, but got no hits in the series and didn't hit a ball out of the infield. Some people never know when it's better not to say anything, especially in this case. He could also be very flaky with horseplay on the field."

"After his playing days were over, he returned to the Cubs as a coach and during World War I served as athletic director at the Great Lakes Naval Training Station in the suburb of North Chicago. They had 48 baseball teams with more than 2,000 players.

"He later became baseball coach at Franklin and Marshall College in Lancaster, PA, for a few years before retiring from the sport he loved so much. Well, that's the end of the story telling for tonight. I'll see what I can come up with for the next game. See you then," Jeff says as he concludes this lesson in Chicago baseball history. (69)

Chapter 15 – Game 5 – October 28, 2016 World Series

"Finally, a day off yesterday after the teams' played five straight days because of the suspended game," Jeff O'Fallon says to his seatmates Katie Sorensen and her husband Tom Buchanan at the White Sox U.S. Cellular Field.

"Now, they've reworked the rest of the schedule so there'll be a day off between each game. So, if it goes to seven, the championship is on November 1st, All Saints Day. How ironic is that?"

Katie quickly chimes in, "I'm trying like crazy to hold off having this baby until after the World Series, but he or she still could come at any moment. I certainly don't want to have a Halloween baby," she adds, then turns to her husband. "We should have thought about it on that cold January night when I got pregnant. It's been worth it though."

"By the way, I can't help but notice how much bigger you've gotten in the past week since we met," Jeff says, turning to Katie. "I don't want to alarm you, but are you sure there's only one Buchanan in there? My daughter and her husband had twins five years ago and there was no indication of more than one child until very late in her pregnancy. They ended up with two girls, each about 4½ pounds. You'd never know they were ever that tiny the way they look now. They're two rapidly growing, very healthy girls, Brooke and Robyn."

"Oh, my God," Katie quickly replies. "It's obvious my stomach has gotten much bigger, actually over the past three weeks. I was just at the doctor two days ago and she didn't say anything. I've told her from the start that we want to be surprised and wait to find out the gender, but if it is twins, I wish she had at least mentioned it! "

"The two ultrasounds I had earlier gave no indication of the possibility of twins and I don't know of any history either in my or Tom's family of twins. Does your daughter live around here. I'd love to talk with her about her last few weeks before they were born?"

"They actually live in Northern California, but I can give you her number and you should call her," Jeff says back to her.

"Don't forget, sweetheart, my father was adopted and he never learned anything about his biological background," Tom adds as they get to their seats.

It's back to the same pitching match-up as in game one with Sale for the Sox and Arrieta on the mound for the Cubs.

Tickets are now going for unimaginable amounts with standing room only access at close to $1,000. The farthest reaches of the upper deck are $2,500 and box seats are easily in the $5,000 price range, or more.

The White Sox take the field on this chilly, but comfortable night and Sale gives an early indication he's on his game with two strikeouts and a pop fly out.

Arrieta also looks very tough for the Cubs with two easy groundouts and follows by striking out Abreu on a nasty curve ball that breaks down and in.

The pitchers dominate until the top of the fourth inning when the Cubs have their hitting shoes on. Rizzo bangs Sale's first pitch down the left field line for a double. He's followed by Bryant who launches a drive to deep right-center field. Eaton gets close, but isn't quite able to catch the ball, then stumbles and briefly falls. By the time right-fielder Garcia rifles a throw toward the infield, Bryant has a stand-up triple.

Designated hitter Kyle Schwarber, batting clean-up in this critical game five, likes the look of Sale's first offering and launches it deep into the right center field bleachers.

Cub fans at the game cheer loudly with this 3-0 lead, though they are relatively few in number compared to the huge number of White Sox fans in their home stadium.

Wrigleyville residents and hundreds of thousands in the Northern and Western suburbs, the majority of them die-hard Cubs supporters, are jumping for joy and nearly ready to start dancing in the streets after the blast off the bat of the Indiana University product.

Schwarber, who has always hit well, is both a catcher and left-fielder. He's the team's backup to Montero this season and also frequently has been called on to play in the outfield and as a pinch-hitter. During interleague games played in American League parks, he's usually the team's designated hitter.

"I can't believe we're on the verge of possibly being down 3 games to 2 in this series heading back to Wrigley with Lester the likely starter," Tom Buchanan utters, obviously very upset over what he is watching as the Cubs put three runs across the plate.

"Relax, Tom. There's no guarantee Arrieta is going to continue to look so good. He's developed into a great pitcher, but there's still enough time for the Sox to string together some hits and score runs," Jeff shoots back. "You have to weigh-in the Cubs history factor. Don't forget what appeared to be a ticket into the 2003 World Series with the devastating Steve Bartman episode."

Who could ever forget it? In the eighth inning of Game 6 of the National League Championship Series with the Cubs ahead 3–0 and holding a 3 games to 2 lead in the best of seven series, several spectators attempted to catch a foul ball off the bat of Florida second baseman Luis Castillo. One of those people in the stands along the left field line, Bartman, a huge lifelong Cubs fan, reached for the ball. He deflected it and disrupted a possible catch by Cubs outfielder Moisés Alou.

If Alou had caught the ball, it would have been the second out in the inning and the Cubs would have been just four outs away from winning their first National League pennant since 1945. Instead, the Cubs ended up surrendering eight runs in the inning and lost the game, 8-3. They were eliminated the next day.

Just as Jeff explains all of that, Cabrera jumps on a pitch from Arrieta and lashes a double into the left field corner. White Sox fans are back to cheering like crazy.

Ramirez watches three pitches sail out of the strike zone for balls, then clumsily swings at a pitch in the dirt and takes two more strikes for the first out. Sanchez lunges at the first offering and pops out weakly in the infield.

That brings up the catcher Vlessen. He looks bad on a slider down and away, not coming close with his weak swing. Then after two balls, he hits a slow ground ball with a weird backspin to third which appears to be a routine play. But Bryant, apparently distracted by Cabrera running toward third, bobbles the ball for an error.

Back to the top of the order for Eaton, who frequently has problems with a tough right- hander like Arrieta. Not this time, though, as he punches a single up the middle to cut the deficit to 3-1 when Cabrera scores.

The fourth inning ends two pitches later after Abreu hits a long fly ball out to left center field.

Arrieta and Sale revert back to near perfection over the next three innings and the score remains 3-1 Cubs after seven. Tension at U.S. Cellular continues to mount.

One of these teams will hold a 3-2 series lead within the next hour or less. If it's the Cubs, they'd be able to wrap it up in two days on their home field. But should the White Sox prevail, they could spoil North Side dreams by winning it all at Wrigley.

Arrieta is determined not to let the latter happen. He strikes out the first two batters in the bottom half of the eighth. Then Thompson, who won game one with a dramatic home run in extra innings, comes up as a pinch hitter and slams a line drive shot into the right center field gap. By the time the ball is retrieved, he's rounding second base and easily reaches third for a triple.

Maddon slowly walks to the mound. Two pitchers have been throwing since the start of the inning, left hander Clayton Richard and right hander Strop. Second baseman Sanchez is the scheduled White Sox hitter. He's been a .248 hitter this season which is an improvement over his .224 average last year as a rookie. But he strikes out way too often.

Maddon signals for Richard, a one-time White Sox starter, who played quarterback on the football field at the University of Michigan. Even though Sanchez is a switch hitter, he's more inclined to make contact left-handed than right-handed. That's seemingly the reason for Maddon's decision.

As for a likely pinch-hitter, the White Sox have had an extremely weak bench the past few years and their manager, Ventura, hasn't been very astute with his decisions when it comes to juggling players.

"He's crazy if he lets Sanchez bat in this situation. Richard will eat him alive," Buchanan shouts out.

"I'm afraid you're right. This isn't a good time to send up a banjo hitter when you need someone with real pop in their bat," O'Fallon quickly replies.

Instead of Sanchez, out comes Courtney Hawkins, the Sox top draft selection four years ago out of Corpus Christi, Texas. He has shown some promise in his ascent through the minor leagues, but is still much too inconsistent as a hitter and average at best as an outfielder.

Hawkins is a big right-handed hitter with plenty of pop in his powerful swing when he's in a good groove. That was the case during the last two weeks of the regular season when he hit four mammoth home runs.

He lays into Richard's first pitch and pulls a long drive far down the left field line, but it curves foul. After two balls, he pops out weakly to second base, leaving the score at 3-1 Cubs heading into the ninth.

Nate Jones strolls in from the bullpen and quickly gets the Cubs out in order. The next relief pitcher on deck for the Cubs is ace closer Hector Rondon to face the top of the White Sox batting order.

Using the theory of trying to get on base in any possible way, Eaton lunges at the first pitch in a feeble bunt attempt. But the only thing he hits is air. Then with a 2-2 count, he lines the ball hard to right field, but the Cubs Soler gets a good jump and snares it.

Abreu quickly has two strikes against him with a weak swing on a pitch down and away, followed by a foul ball. After running the count full at 3-2, the Sox slugger finds a pitch very much to his liking and launches it deep into right center. When it lands 10 rows back into the bleachers, half of the city erupts. It's now 3-2 with one out in the bottom of the ninth.

Maddon again slowly approaches the mound and begins talking with Rondon.

"Tell him to get these last two outs quickly, before I have my baby." Katie shouts out.

"You're not having contractions or anything like that, are you honey?" Tom asks.

"No, not yet, but they could start at any moment and I desperately want to be around for the end of this World Series," Katie adds. "I'm truly beginning to believe that the Cubs are going to win the whole thing, in six games!"

"We'll see about that, won't we?" Tom sarcastically says back to her.

At that moment, Rondon goes into his windup against Cabrera. It's ball one, followed by a called strike, then a swinging strike. Another ball is next bringing the count to 2-2.

The pitch after that is lined down toward the right field corner, with two bases written all over it, but just hooks foul at the last possible moment.

The Wrigley faithful city-wide breathe a huge sigh of relief when he eventually pops out to Castro near second base.

Now the noise level at U.S. Cellular Field is at a record level as designated hitter Adam LaRoche steps into the batter's box. He fouls off the first two pitches and then expects the third pitch to be low, but home plate umpire Salvatore Duzzi loudly yells, "Strike three, you're out!"

Baseball's so-called loveable losers, the Chicago Cubs, are now within one game of winning the World Series over their crosstown rivals, the Chicago White Sox.

The last time they were this close was in 1945 when their World War II series went seven games against the Detroit Tigers.

The Cubs trailed 3 games to 2, with the last two games scheduled in Wrigley Field because of wartime scheduling adjustments to cut down on the amount of travel involved.

It took 12 innings before the Cubs squeezed out an 8-7 win on a double by third baseman Stan Hack off Tigers pitcher Dizzy Trout.

That tied the series at 3 with the Cubs set to play game seven at home. Optimism ran high, despite the ongoing war with its many casualties. But the Cubs were basically finished before they ever came to bat as the Tigers scored five runs in the top-half of the first inning on the way to a 9-3 win.

The big hit was a bases clearing double by catcher Paul Richards, who later became the White Sox manager for several years in the 1950s and again in 1976.

There also was an 18-year-old kid on the Tigers roster who longtime White Sox fans will never forget. Left-hander Billy Pierce was a mainstay of the Sox pitching corps from 1949 through 1961 when he was traded to the San Francisco Giants.

He won 211 games during a brilliant career that included two 20-game seasons with the Sox in 1956 and 1957. Pierce also helped lead the White Sox to the 1959 World Series and the Giants into the 1962 fall classic.

His career earned run average was 3.27 and he had 193 complete games and 38 shutouts. Those last two numbers alone are fantastic.

He also helped himself with a bat in a number of games, with 203 hits, 13 doubles, 4 triples and 69 runs batted in, long before the designated hitter rule.

Billy Pierce later worked for many years in community relations with the White Sox.

He died at the age of 88 in July, 2015. It was news that greatly saddened thousands of former players who competed against him as well as the millions of fans from coast to coast who cheered his many accomplishments on the pitchers' mound.

Chapter 16 – Game 6 – October 14, 1906 World Series

Nearly 20,000 people were on hand at South Side Park for what White Sox fans hoped would be the final game of the 1906 World Series.

Back on their home field, the Sox sent Doc White to the mound against future Hall of Famer Mordecai "Three Finger" Brown for the Cubs. White was pitching on just one day of rest, similar to what "Big Ed" Walsh of the Sox had previously done.

The Cubs wasted no time scoring in this critical game. A double by Wildfire Schulte in the top of the first gave the Cubs as early lead. But any hopes they had of tying up the series faded quickly when George Davis and Jiggs Donahue hit back to back doubles, driving in three runs and giving the Sox a 3-1 lead after just one inning.

The onslaught continued with two out in the second for the home team. "Noodles" Hahn singled and Fielder Jones walked. Then Frank Isbell, Davis and Rohe each had a base-knock. Combine that with another walk and a botched double play attempt and four more runs had crossed the plate. Brown lasted less than two innings and the Cubs trailed 7-1.

The rest of the contest was indeed quite uneventful. The Cubs pushed across a run in the fifth on a groundout and the Sox added another tally in the bottom of the eighth.

It became interesting in the ninth when the Cubs pushed across another run to make it 8-3 with the bases loaded. But Schulte grounded out to first and the game and the World Series were history!

The White Sox, known throughout baseball as the hitless wonders, had won the World Series, 4 games to 2.

Statistics showed they remained hitless wonders during the series, batting just .198. The Cubs, on the other hand, weren't much better at .196. A good portion of the White Sox sudden emergence as hitters came in games five and six when they pounded out 26 hits after previously only managing nine during the first four games.

White Sox outfielder Patsy Dougherty became the first player ever to both play in and win two World Series. He had previously been a member of the Boston Americans in the 1903 event.

From a financial standpoint, the White Sox winning player's share was $1,875 per man compared to the Cubs' losing share of $440. (70)

Consider that against the payouts for the 2014 World Series. Each player on the winning San Francisco Giants received $388,606 while Kansas City Royals players took home $230,700. Not a bad piece of change! (71)

"After all the struggles with weather in 1906, the "Hitless Wonders" won game six in that very decisive manner. The winning pitcher for the Pale Hose had something in common with another player I told you about earlier, Frank Owen. Guy "Doc" White also had a medical-type degree. He was a dentist and earned his dental surgery degree from Georgetown University in 1902, " O'Fallon begins.

"Soon after that he signed with the Phillies before jumping to the White Sox in 1903. He became the pitching ace for the team right after he joined the Sox. In September, 1904, he set a record which stood for 64 years when he threw five consecutive shutouts and a total of six for the month. He also held a record which will be hard to break, 45 consecutive scoreless innings that year! White pitched in relief for the Sox during the 1906 series and started only game six for the South Siders and became a big hero for the team when he threw the final game for the White Sox victory."

"Being a master of always knowing where his pitches were going was the key to White's success. He threw a very tricky curve ball and was a complete control pitcher, once going 65 innings without issuing a walk," says Jeff.

"Of course, there was more to his life. In the off-season he practiced dentistry for a few years and closed his practice in 1906 to concentrate on baseball. Who knows, he might actually have practiced on his teammates during the season. There's nothing like having a physician and dentist traveling with you, especially in those days. In addition, he was a violinist, singer and songwriter."

"To add to his interesting life, he supposedly became an evangelical minister and traveled the Chautauqua circuit in upstate New York. With his record and statistics, he should be in the Hall of Fame, but unfortunately that never happened. By the way, the pitcher who broke his shutout record in 1968

is in the Hall of Fame ….Don Drysdale," ends Jeff.
(72)

"Our last 1906 player to tell you about is Cubs right fielder Frank Schulte, nicknamed "Wildfire."

"The nickname wasn't only for his energy on the field. One night a few Cubs players went to see a play starring Lillian Russell, the very popular and beautiful star of that era, in Vicksburg, Mississippi. Schulte admired her and actually got to meet her at a party after the play. The other ball fielders called him "Wildfire," the name of the play they saw that evening.

"According to the family story, Schulte got the name because he wouldn't stop talking about her or the drama," explains Jeff.

"Schulte came up with the Cubs in 1904 and stayed through 1916. In his first start, he filled in for the regular third baseman and got three hits, including a triple in the first game of a double header and two more in the second."

"He also stole home 22 times during his career and became a fixture on the team. He had many eccentricities, like looking for hairpins on the street. He claimed they predicted his success in the batter's box in the upcoming game."

"The bigger the hairpin he found, the better he would hit. He also blamed his shoes for batting slumps and used a very thin-handled 40 ounce bat. For that time, when bats seldom shattered, he broke an extraordinary number because of the thin handle."

"Besides playing baseball, he owned race horses, even naming one of them "Wildfire" after the Lillian Russell play," continues Jeff.

"'Wildfire' played in four World Series and had a .309 lifetime average during those championship runs. He also had a 13 game hitting streak which tied him in fourth place all-time with Harry Hooper and Deter Jeter."

"He was also the first player to hit four grand slams in one season, hit for the cycle and in another game had a homer and double in the same inning. It's been passed down to me that my great-great-great grandfather considered him not only a wonderful ball player, but an interesting and unusual person who he came to cherish knowing and greatly respecting for many years."

"Schulte finished his career in the Pacific Coast League with the Oakland Oaks. He and his wife settled down in Oakland where he lived for the remainder of his life," states Jeff. (73)

"The next time we meet, I'll tell you about my great-great-great grandfather, Patrick O'Shea, who was the person who started the tradition of passing on the stories about the teams and people during his life as a sports writer in Chicago. See you then and Katie, I hope you will still be around to go to the game. Let me know if it might be twins. When do you next see your doctor?" asks O'Fallon.

"I go tomorrow for a check-up, but I'm planning on being at the next game. The baby or babies will just have to wait until we know who the World Series winner is," Katie insists.

Chapter 17 – Off Day – October 29, 2016 World Series

It's a media frenzy unlike anything seen in Chicago for many years, even decades.

There had been enormous crowds after championships in the modern electronic era, like the Bears winning the Super Bowl in 1986, or the Bulls' six titles in 1991-93 and again from 1996-98, the Blackhawks' three Stanley Cups in 2010, 2013 and 2015 or, of course, the White Sox World Series title in 2005.

In each of those championship years, television camera crews beyond those from local Chicago stations have been seen, but nothing similar to the mass of world-wide media on hand this year.

Even on this off-day between games 5 and 6, there are satellite trucks aplenty surrounding Wrigley Field. The Cubs are going through a short workout on their home field at 10am, while the White Sox have similar plans for a 2pm workout at their home ballpark. Many of these trucks will make the rushed trip from 3600

North to 3500 South for the afternoon workout and rounds of interviews.

Reporters are crowding around Cubs players, Maddon and top executives firing away with non-stop questions. The team could potentially win the World Series on their home field in just over 30 hours from now.

The pitching match-ups for tomorrow's game are only partially known. Maddon is definitely planning to start Lester, who has plenty of World Series experience and brilliance with the Red Sox.

Sox manager Ventura, on the other hand, is playing it very coy and refuses to commit to a definite starter between Rodon and Johnson.

"We'll consider all the match-ups and possibilities and come up with a decision," he tells the somewhat frustrated mass of reporters without giving any hints. "They've each had some success this season against their crosstown rivals."

Rodon also was less than effective in another start against the Cubs during the regular season. He only lasted four innings while giving up five runs in one of his least impressive performances. The White Sox did come back to win that game 9-5, but he was not the pitcher of record.

He's also excited about the possibility of batting in this game at Wrigley, with no designated hitter in the lineup for either team since it's at a National League park.

"My main focus is on getting batters out, but I like the idea of possibly also batting. I was a fairly decent hitter in college. We'll just see what happens," Rodon, who hit .267 (20 for 75) during his days at North Carolina State, explains. (74)

Veteran Chicago sports television anchors-reporters Mark Giangreco of ABC7 (WLS-TV) and Dan Roan of WGN9 cannot believe the large turnout of media from every imaginable part of the world.

"Even nations that barely know the game of baseball, much less having played it, are here reporting every aspect of what's happening. That certainly tells you how highly regarded Chicago is as a world class city," Giangreco says. "In all the years I've been involved in day to day sports coverage, this is the most incredible thing I've ever experienced."

"The entire world is fascinated by the fact that these two longtime baseball teams in the same large city have only played one other time for the championship and that was 110 years ago," Roan adds.

Tickets for tomorrow's game six at Wrigley are priced through the roof. If you think $25,000 has been an outrageous amount to pay for a Super Bowl game or NBA championship match-up in the past, try again. Sources tell us that some seats for games 6 and 7, if there is a game 7, may easily reach $50,000 each!

The weather on this off day in unpredictable Chicago is gorgeous, very much like Indian summer. The daytime temperature is 65 degrees with bright sunshine and a slight breeze. But beware of an approaching cold front and strong chance of heavy rain for tomorrow's game 6!

Chapter 18 – Game 6 – October 30, 2016 World Series

Chicago baseball players and millions of residents wake up to heavy rain pounding down on the city with very chilly, blustery winds as everyone braces for game 6 of the 2016 World Series.

The weather forecast is a bit more encouraging than what we're seeing this morning. It calls for the rain to move out of the area by noon and winds to taper down. Tonight's temperature is expected to be in the mid-50s with more of a slight breeze than blowing skies.

Meantime, a thousand miles away in New York, Commissioner Rob Manfred is conducting a major conference call with his top executives, the biggest brass of the White Sox and Cubs, along with the major television honchos from the WOLF network.

The subject: considering whether to move a possible game 7 from November 1st back to October 31th . Manfred is concerned about Chicago's very uncertain weather and would prefer not to have the season extend into November.

The teams are relatively agreeable, but WOLF is very adamant about there being no change. They have scheduled a big night of Halloween spooky and scary programming, which has been heavily promoted and advertised, already showing up as a likely huge success in the ratings and demos.

"All the time sold for that game is based on the date and we'd have to do an incredible job of juggling everything," a top WOLF vice president explains. "If we don't want baseball on Halloween, I guess we all have to root our asses off for the Cubs to wrap it up tonight."

When the White Sox executives hear this during the call, they explode and implore Manfred to do something about it. He says he will give it some thought and tells everyone that WOLF has too much at stake and the schedule will remain the way it is.

Sox manager Ventura says he's finally ready to announce his starting pitcher and will tell the world who it is at a 1pm news conference. To no one's surprise, it winds up being Rodon who will face the Cubs and now oppose Lester.

Ventura also emphasizes that all hands will be ready to come in to pitch. And that includes the likes of Johnson, Quintana and even Sale, if needed.

Meantime, Katie and Tom meet up with their new found friend Jeff for a bite to eat before the game and there is news about their situation to ponder.

"I went to the doctor yesterday. She listened again very attentively with a stethoscope and thought she might have heard two heartbeats this time. She even had another doctor in the office also listen and he was more convinced, but not sure. We'll just have to wait and see," Katie explains. "She also added that she didn't think the baby would be born for a few more days. So if there is a game seven, hopefully not, I should be able to attend, although right now I'm getting anxious to find out if it's twins or not."

"If there is a second baby, I guess he or she is hiding. I did a lot of research on the computer after I got home from the doctor's office and learned that while it's unusual, there have been many women who didn't find out until very late in their pregnancy or even in the delivery room."

"One woman said she found out at 28 weeks. They were hiding behind one another. A second woman was 30 weeks along. It's all very bizarre," she concludes.

"It's also unbelievable that we've spent a lot of money on a crib, a bassinette, changing table, buggy, car seat, diapers and clothing. Now we may have to double that amount! Our apartment isn't that large and it'll be very crowded," Tom laments. "Whatever Katie has is fine with us as long as he, she or they are healthy!"

"Thank you again, Jeff, for commenting on how much bigger I have gotten in such a short time," Katie chimes in.

"Let me know if there's anything I can do to help you. We've only known each other for a short time, but I feel like you're almost family. You remind me in many ways of my daughter and her husband," Jeff replies.

"Thanks a lot. Let's just worry right now about this ballgame. Let's get to our seats and see what happens," Katie responds.

The Cubs and all their supporters, both in Wrigley Field and elsewhere around the world, have visions of a title after Lester retires the side in order in the top of the first and the team's hitters immediately begin to peck away at Rodon.

Each of his first two pitches is lined for singles by Fowler and Rizzo.

"Way to go Cubbies. Let's get a bunch of runs early so Jon can just put it on automatic pilot and glide home," Katie yells out. She's now bigger than ever as the birth of her first-born child draws nearer and nearer.

Sox pitching coach Don Cooper is already on the mound talking with Rodon, obviously trying to get him to calm down and stay more focused.

This situation might normally call for a bunt to get the runners into scoring position in such a critical game, but Bryant hasn't attempted a sacrifice all season and doesn't appear ready to lay one down now. In fact, he takes a ferocious swing at the first pitch and tops a weak ground ball foul down the third base line.

The next two pitches are balls, followed by a swinging strike to even the count at 2-2. Then he's fooled by a change-up pitch and softly pops out to Abreu in foul territory by the first base bag.

Soler is next and Rodon is reinvigorated by pitching so effectively to Bryant. He quickly blows two strikes, on a fast ball and slider, past the Cubs third baseman, then badly fools him on a change-up which he grounds to third base. That's quickly turned into an around- the-horn double play.

In fact, Soler takes a bad step after crossing the bag at first and is suddenly limping. He's eventually replaced in right field by rookie Chico Vaughn.

"So the Cubs couldn't quite get the big hit they needed so badly," Tom blares out after turning to his unhappy wife. "Now watch the White Sox string together a few hits and get this series evened up."

He's partially correct when Cabrera reaches out and lines the second pitch into the left field corner for a double. Then LaRoche wastes little time laying down a good sacrifice bunt to first baseman Rizzo.

It's a man on third and one out for Avisail Garcia. Throughout the season with runners in scoring position, like Cabrera is now, Garcia has hit an impressive .315. Overall, his average is .272 with far too many strikeouts.

Lester is determined not to let this run score and gets two quick strikes on the batter. After a border-line pitch that Garcia lets go by him on the inside corner is called a ball, he digs in and gets ready for something he can drive to the outfield. That's exactly what happens as he lifts a high fly ball to Fowler in medium center field.

Cabrera tags and makes a mad dash to home plate, just beating the strong throw with a nifty slide around the catcher to give the White Sox a 1-0 lead.

"That was a real good throw home. It's a good thing for the Sox that Cabrera knows how to maneuver his body so he can just get his hand on the plate an instant before he's tagged," Jeff tells Tom and Katie.

Maddon appeals the decision by umpire Moe East and the electronic replay shows he's barely safe, just the way the play had been called. Maddon has another motive, however, for appealing the play.

He's livid about the pitch on the inside corner that East called a ball during Garcia's at bat and begins to give the oft-controversial umpire a piece of his mind over what he considers a blown call that should have been a strikeout.

Since managers and coaches aren't allowed to question balls and strikes calls, he's immediately ejected from the game once again and Wrigley Field is a crescendo of loud booing for several minutes.

"That's such a typical Maddon move. He's an absolute master of intimidation and motivation. This is intended to get his ball club fired up, as well as to warn East and the other five umpires that they'd better be at their very best for the rest of the game and the series, as well," Jeff adds.

Lester gets the final out of the second inning, but Rodon is much stronger in the bottom half and easily retires the Cubs on just eight pitches.

Two more scoreless innings quickly go by without any baserunners for either team and by the end of four, the score remains 1-0. It's another true nail-biter with so much at stake for each team.

In the top of the fifth, the White Sox are handed what might best be described as a gift from God or a few Christmas/Hanukkah presents to end all holiday presents. It begins innocently enough when Eaton beats out a bunt toward third. That is followed by another bunt, this time an intended sacrifice, by third baseman Saladino.

As it snakes its way along the third base line, Bryant is sure it will go foul, so he lets it roll and roll some more but it never turns left toward the foul line. Not only is Saladino already at first, but now Eaton is racing toward third base with no one there to take a throw. Shortstop Russell is still parked at his regular position between second and third with nary a move toward third. Two men on and no one out.

Abreu is next and on the third pitch lofts a high fly ball to right field which Vaughn somehow misjudges in the lights and next thing you know, he's holding his hands out to his side with seemingly no clue as to where the ball is. Turns out he's a good ten feet from the ball where it safely drops

Eaton easily scores from third and Saladino knows that Vaughn is in big trouble and just starts running and doesn't stop until he crosses home plate. That makes it 3-0 and Abreu ends up on third with a stand-up triple.

Lester is beside himself on the mound and stomps around in disgust, eventually also throwing the rosin bag down in frustration. Pitching coach Bosio comes out from the dugout to try and calm him down, hoping he can get his focus back.

That thought quickly goes away when LaRoche flies out to deep center and Abreu easily trots home with the Sox fourth run. There's a very uneasy calm among the Cubs faithful, including Katie, when Garcia tops off the inning with a long home run blast onto Waveland Avenue.

"Unbelievable!" cries out Katie. "I can't believe all of that just happened and now we're trailing 5-0. It looks like there will be baseball in November and we'll have to go back to U.S. Cellular for it."

The Cubs have the bottom of the order up and are as shell shocked at the plate as they were in the field during the top half of the inning, going up and down in order.

So now we move on to the top of the sixth and Lester returns to the mound, but doesn't last much longer.

The White Sox suddenly seem to have their hitting shoes on and rattle off three very solid hits, doubles by Cabrera and Ramirez, followed by a single off the bat of Vlessen. It's now a 7-0 football-like score on this cool night that's very football-like in nature.

Lester is finished for the night and so are some Cubs fans. They slowly begin to head for the exits and are taunted and jeered by the thousands of die-hards still on hand.

"The idiots who are leaving obviously aren't true Cubs fans," Jeff says as he turns toward Katie and Tom. "I'm surprised this many people are packing it in when it's still relatively early in the game.

"If the situation were reversed in terms of the score, I'm not sure if White Sox bandwagon people wouldn't be doing the same thing," Tom chimes in. "But, assuming this score holds up, I'm delighted there will be a game seven. It's the greatest thing imaginable for our wonderful city."

"Yes, that's for certain!" Katie adds. "But I'm not giving up yet on this game. We all know how capable the Cubs are of bunching hits together and scoring a lot of runs."

"Not tonight, sweetheart," Tom replies, leaning over and giving Katie a big kiss accompanied by a huge hug.

That moment of passion is suddenly interrupted when Cubs left fielder and occasional catcher Schwarber hits a long two-run home run to right field in the bottom of the 6th to now make it a 7-2 game.

Rodon struggles to finish up the inning and speculation is strong that he's done for the night after throwing 98 pitches during his six innings of work.

The White Sox are looking for more runs in the top of the 7th against new Cubs pitcher Clayton Richard. Eaton bloops a double down the left field line to lead things off and then is sacrificed to third with one out.

Next is Abreu who takes two pitches, a strike and ball, then unloads a monster shot, deep into Wrigley's center field bleachers, bringing the score to 9-2 and activating a true mass move by Cubs fans to exits in all areas of the ballpark.

"Wow, what a blast," Tom says as he leans toward Katie and Jeff. "He's been a good player for us these past three years, but sometimes gets into these hitting funks and you wonder if he's ever going to get back his groove. Hopefully, he'll have it for game seven and will be ready to bring the Sox the championship in two nights. A White Sox title and the World Series MVP award for Mr. Abreu. I'm all for both."

"We'll see about that," Katie turns back to him with a terse reply. "Assuming the Sox hold onto this big lead tonight and are able to win, game seven and the hype surrounding it should provide us with one of the most incredible nights in Chicago's long and remarkable history. I'm just thrilled that we'll be part of it. Our child or children will relish the moment once they learn about it."

"I don't know about you, but as big of a White Sox fan I've been my entire life, I'm almost at the point where I'm just thrilled for what a great spectacle this World Series has been for the City of Chicago," Tom bluntly says. "I certainly want the Sox to win, but if they don't, it wouldn't be the end of the world for me. My biggest concern is seeing the newest member or members of our family."

"That's very sweet of you to say and it makes me love you more and more every day," Katie turns to him and says, then gives him another big hug and kiss.

The game seems to take forever to finish. The Cubs kept pecking away, cutting the lead to 9-4 in the bottom of the seventh, this time on a two-run dinger by Chris Denorfia over the high screen in left field and onto Waveland against Zach Putnam.

That results in Putnam's hasty exit as left-hander Zach Duke enters from the bullpen to face Rizzo, who hits the ball hard, but right at second baseman Sanchez for the third out to end the inning.

After the White Sox meekly go out in order in the top of the eighth, the Cubs show the 30,000 plus remaining fans they want to end the World Series tonight.

It begins innocently enough with a bunt single by Vaughn and when Schwarber makes big-time contact again with a line drive off the right field wall, there now are runners on second and third with no one out and the crowd is in frenzy.

"I told you the Cubs would likely come back. Too bad for all those saps who left early. They're missing this," Katie loudly exclaims turning to Tom as new Sox pitcher Matt Albers walks in from the bullpen.

"I'm not surprised as inconsistent as our bullpen has been lately. Even if the Sox hold on here and win, I just hope they don't have to use our closer David Robertson tonight. He needs to be in tip-top shape for a game seven, if there is one," Tom replies to her.

Albers' first pitch to Chris Coghlan only travels about 58 feet and bounces past Vlessen, bringing home Vaughn and sending Schwarber to third. It's now 9-5 and soon becomes 9-6 on a long sacrifice fly to center fielder Eaton.

After the second out, it's back to the top of the order and Fowler keeps the rally going with a single up the middle. That brings manager Ventura to the mound. Normally pitching coach Don Cooper comes out for the first visit with a pitcher in peril.

But no, Ventura is there and it's apparent he's far from thrilled. After another minute of delivering a tongue-lashing to Albers, he signals to the bullpen to bring in Robertson after all.

Rizzo is up next and intensely studies the relief pitcher as he delivers his warmup tosses. The batter knows this pitcher quite well. He hit two home runs off him during inter-league games this season, one being a game-winner which cost Rodon a victory.

He's ready for the first pitch and lines it hard down the right field line, but it curves foul. A huge buzz goes through the very excited and electrified crowd. They can sense and smell a potential come from behind win and the team's first World Series title in 108 years, since 1908.

The next two pitches are balls, but Robertson totally disagrees and yells his displeasure in the direction of home plate umpire Moe East. Ventura, who is normally very stoic and laid back, is beside himself in the dugout.

Rizzo sees the next delivery coming and has it on his radar from the instant it leaves the pitcher's hand. He's determined to hit it a long, long way and takes a mighty swing.

But his bat undercuts the ball, not quite making a perfect connection. He still hits it a long way, but high in the air instead of as a line drive and is eventually caught by Eaton in front of the center field wall.

A very huge sigh of relief is heard coming from White Sox fans throughout the ballpark as well as around the city and throughout the nation.

This game though is still far from over as the White Sox come to bat in the top of the ninth against relief pitcher Omar (Turk) Lown III. He's the great-grandson of a former Chicago pitcher for both teams who was a member of the 1959 pennant winning White Sox. The original Turk Lown was primarily a middle inning reliever who had 55 wins and 73 saves during his 11 year career.

Lown gives up a leadoff single to Vlessen and the Sox bunt him to second, but are unable to bring him home.

So now it's onto the bottom of the ninth with Bryant leading off against Robertson.

He takes two balls, then absolutely pulverizes the next pitch, off the video board in left field for a home run to make the score 9-7. The drive is estimated to have traveled 463 feet, a true monster blast like so many of the long home runs he has hit since becoming a Cub. One more baserunner brings up the tying run.

Katie is in ecstasy jumping up down while Tom is frantically trying to get her to calm down, fearing she might be ready to deliver at any second.

"Please, honey, just take it easy. I know how excited you and all the Cubs fans are," Tom pleads with her.

"But we could win the World Series right here, right now," she excitedly yells back.

Robertson regains his composure though and gets the next three hitters out on a lazy fly ball and two strikeouts. The Sox have won 9-7 to tie the series at three games each and bring the decisive contest back to U.S. Cellular Field.

"That certainly was something," Jeff says to the young couple after the game. "Robertson was very lucky on that ball Rizzo hit. He just missed hitting it out. Our closer needs to have better stuff if he's called on in game seven or it could be curtains for the White Sox."

"That's for sure," Tom replies. "The way the Cubs came back, I'm just happy the White Sox managed to hold on. The Cubs truly hit the pee out of the ball in the last few innings."

"Well, I'll see you both in two days for the big game. Let me get your phone number and I'll give you mine. Please keep me posted if there is anything to report on the baby situation," Jeff concludes as they hug one another before heading for home.

Chapter 19 – "Halloween Tricks & Treats"– October 31, 2016

Because of the weird schedule after game one was suspended following the huge storm, there was an off day between games five and six and now games six and seven.

That's the way Major League Baseball reworked the schedule even though the games are being played just a few miles apart with virtually no travel involved.

Now it's a matter of nervously waiting it out for the city and the entire country to determine who will emerge as Chicago's Champions of the World.

Plans have been made for each team's parade route. The gigantic celebratory event will be held November 2nd, the day after game seven.

In either case, the parade will start at the winner's home ballpark, either Wrigley Field or U.S. Cellular Field aka Comiskey Park.

From there, it weaves through several neighborhoods until reaching downtown. At that point, it will proceed down Dearborn Street and wind up at the Daley Plaza Center for a gigantic rally and trophy presentation next to the huge statue by Picasso.

Mayor Rahm Emanuel has been lobbying for a parade that would honor both teams, regardless who wears the crown, but was overruled by baseball protocol and tradition.

Walking through the city, there's a lot of preparedness going on along both potential parade routes. Streets are being cleaned up, signs and banners being hung from light posts, red white and blue banners with huge White Sox and Cubs logos are being put in place and there's a feeling of euphoria even though the champion has yet to be decided.

Barricades to be used for crowd control have been delivered to numerous locations where people will flock to watch the gigantic parade. Days off for Chicago police officers and firefighters have been canceled for both the night of the game as well as the following day's parade.

Special service on Metra commuter railroad lines, the Chicago Transit Authority's subway and elevated lines and bus service throughout the city and suburbs is being arranged with appropriate signs put in place.

The local news media is in a frenzy getting together additional video pieces for television and special audio reports for radio to add to its wall to wall live coverage.

That part includes determining camera locations for not only the parade, but also favorite watering holes and celebratory venues.

To no one's surprise, the starting pitchers for game seven have been announced and they are Hendricks for the Cubs, winner of game two, and the White Sox will use Johnson, the victor in game three.

Cubs and Sox merchandise is flying off store shelves, both the legal Major League Baseball approved items as well as bootlegged, less expensive illegal versions.

People worldwide have become instant fans of both teams, more so the Cubs, for years known as Chicago's Lovable Losers even though, in reality, the White Sox haven't fared much better!

Chapter 20 – Game 7 – November 1, 2016 World Series

Jeff rushes up as he spies Katie and Tom waiting for him in front of U.S. Cellular Field. The first day of November in Chicago is cool and brisk, signs of winter not being too far away.

"Katie, it's great to see that you made it to game seven. Let's go inside, find some place to get a bite to eat and I'll tell you about my great-great-great grandfather, Patrick O'Shea, and how he got to be a reporter for the *Chicago Gazette*," Jeff O'Fallon says.

"That sounds great, Jeff, but I'm not feeling really great right now, so I think I'll skip the food, get something to drink and listen some more to your fascinating stories."

They join the rush of fans getting into the park, even though the final game of the series won't start for nearly three hours. Whether the people entering are White Sox or Cubs fans, everyone is very nervous about the outcome. It's been a wonderful series so far and each side is worried about leaving without a championship.

Finding a comfortable, quiet place to sit is not easy, but they manage to find a cozy nook under the stands along the third base line. As Katie and Tom eat and drink, Jeff begins his tale of Patrick O'Shea.

"As you may remember, he was born during the Great Chicago Fire. The story is Patrick was fascinated by historical events and was always trying to find newspapers, usually those left behind by others, since his family often did not have the money to buy their own copy, even though they only cost a few pennies," Jeff explains.

"In those days, it was more common for children to not finish school. They left before the eighth grade to go out and work to help their families survive. Young Patrick was lucky. Because he only had one brother and one sister and his father had a good job, he could finish grammar school and even attend high school."

"His grades were good and he applied for admission to Chicago Manual High School which opened in 1884 at the corner of Michigan Avenue and 12th Street, now Roosevelt Road, the year before he graduated from eighth grade."

"Chicago Manual was established to teach students a trade. In recent years, those types of schools have pretty much faded away. He entered the printing program which is one of the reasons he was able to get a job at the *Chicago Gazette* after his education."

"The *Gazette* was a less well known paper than the *Tribune, Daily News or The Sun.* He was hired at the paper as a copy boy, mostly getting coffee or pencils or other needed items for the editors and reporters. He also loved to write and would watch the reporters when he could and see what they were putting together and how they did it. He knew that's what he wanted to do with his life.

He began writing stories on his own and one day a reporter asked to see his work. The reporter was impressed and showed it to the editor. Since the paper was short of reporters at that time, my great-great-great grandfather was promoted. His beat was usually smaller, less important local stories, but it was great training for him."

"Wow!" yells Tom, "Patrick seems like a very determined young man who knew what he wanted to do and really pursued it. That's wonderful. You must be very proud of him."

"Yes, I am," replies Jeff, "He's an icon in our family history."

"Let me go on. Just about that time, "yellow journalism" was rearing its head in the newspaper business. Under the auspices of William Randolph Hearst, newspapers began writing not necessarily factual articles, but sensational ones sometimes even making up the information. It started in New York City over competition for readers, but soon swept through the country."

"This form of journalism and the owners drive to make the most money is believed by many to have provoked the Spanish-American War. It's believed they made up some information about the sinking of the United States battleship Maine in Havana Harbor in 1898. They claimed the Cubans did it, but people think the ship was sunk by Americans to start a war."

"Because Patrick was single and the youngest reporter, he was sent to cover the war. Cuba was not an easy place to be. Diseases, insects and various kinds of critters were very prevalent, which is why more experienced reporters did not want to go there."

"Once there, he covered the story following Roosevelt and his Rough Riders as they fought battles. He was even at the Battle of San Juan Hill, which made Roosevelt famous! "

"That was the last time he covered anything like that. Patrick was a very good amateur baseball player as an outfielder and loved the game."

"In 1901, when Charles Comiskey brought the White Sox to Chicago, he managed to get himself assigned to cover them. By the next year, he was also reporting on the Cubs. In those days, reporters did not travel with the teams, so he could handle both of them."

"My grandfather would tell me about going to games with his father and grandfather. Everyone seemed to know Patrick and be in awe of him because of his contribution to sports reporting and his knowledge of the game. I'm very proud of my great-great-great grandfather and what he achieved in life," Jeff concludes.

"That's wonderful. What an impressive family you come from. I wish I could have met him or at least have known more about him," says Katie.

"Thanks so much for the nice words. I guess we need to finish up and get to our seats. The biggest game in decades in Chicago is about to begin in a few minutes. I think we're sitting near each other tonight so I'll check in on you during the game to see how you're feeling, Katie."

"I'm actually going to the first aid station where the paramedics are located to let them know about Katie's situation," Tom tells Jeff and Katie. "Hopefully we won't have to worry about it during the game, but I want to make certain they know exactly where we are if we have to call them."

"I'm feeling pretty good right now although whoever is in my stomach, he, she or they, has been very active these past couple of days. Someone is ready to join the real world and I'm looking forward to it!" Katie chuckles.

"We drove to the ballpark tonight instead of taking the 'L' train. That's just in case we need to get out of here in a hurry to go to the hospital," Tom tells Jeff.

"If you need to leave in a hurry, text me so I'll know. I'm sitting just two sections away, closer to home plate, and if you end up going by ambulance, I'd be happy to bring your car to you at Mercy Hospital so it won't have to sit here at the ballpark overnight, or get towed away," Jeff offers. "After all, Mercy Hospital is less than two miles from here and I came to the game by train."

In a matter of just a few hours, a new World Series champion will also be sitting on top of the real world and that team will represent Chicago, regardless of whether it's the Cubs or White Sox.

The White Sox take the field amid a thunderous roar of approval from the standing room only U.S. Cellular Field crowd. This decisive game could be played in a stadium that seats 400,000, instead of just over 40,000, top baseball and television executives say, and there still would be a huge demand for tickets and huge money made off the television broadcast.

In fact at WFLD-TV, the local WOLF network station in Chicago, a 30-second commercial time slot for a local product or company costs nearly a half-million dollars for the final game of the World Series, according to *Advertising Age* magazine.

That's more than the average cost of a 30-second television spot for Sunday Night Football's average estimate of $415,000. (75) A Super Bowl commercial is the ultimate in terms of cost, in the vicinity of $4.5 million. (76)

The World Series figure is surprisingly high almost every year, just under the price tag for ads run during the Oscars and finales of popular television series.

All the business aspects notwithstanding, it's time to play ball!

The Cubs are very upbeat during batting practice and warmups prior to this colossal game. That reflects Maddon's positive attitude during his first two years as the team's manager.

And that doesn't lessen once the game starts.

Fowler leads off with a beautiful drag bunt single that freezes pitcher Johnson and first baseman Abreu to cheers from Cubs fans throughout the city.

Rizzo then fakes another bunt, but takes two pitches for balls. The third pitch he sees is as delectable to him as a big piece of chocolate cake. He lashes it deep into left-center field, all the way to the wall and by the time Eaton tracks it down, Fowler is crossing home plate with the game's first run and Rizzo is on third before many people are even seated.

Bryant's hard single to left field follows and very quickly it is a 2-0 game.

Before this decisive contest ever starts, both Ventura and Maddon make it clear that amid such high drama, everyone will be available. Once Bryant's hit flies off his bat, it doesn't take long for

White Sox pitching ace Sale to start warming up, along with right handed relief pitcher Jake Petricka.

"With Johnson, you never know for certain if you're going to get a gem or a God-awful performance," Tom angrily says. "He's only a little more than a few years off a college campus. I'm glad to see they've already got Sale warming up. He certainly could go several innings, maybe even five, just like the Giants' Madison Bumgarner did in game 7 of the 2014 World Series."

"Don't forget how the Arizona Diamondbacks used both of their aces, Curt Schilling and Randy Johnson, in game seven when they beat the Yankees 3-2 to wrap up the 2001 World Series," Katie adds.

"That was one helluva series, not only from a baseball standpoint, but even more importantly in helping the nation heal somewhat from the tragedy that occurred on September 11th. There was still much more healing to be done over a long period of time, but that was a good starting point," answers Tom."

Johnson finally gets the side out in the top of the first inning, trailing by two runs.

Now it's the White Sox turn against Hendricks, but their bats are super-silent. Eaton, Saladino and Cabrera are all easy outs on just a total of 11 pitches.

Johnson is more on his game in the second. He gives up a harmless single to left fielder Schwarber, but gets all three outs via the strikeout route with the batters overmatched and taking wild swings at pitches in the dirt.

"Now it's our turn to make some noise," Tom speculates as the bottom of the second begins. "Hendricks is a good pitcher, but I think we'll be able to time his fastball real well either this inning or very soon."

No more than a few seconds after he says that, Trayce Thompson launches a long drive into right center field. There's no doubt about this blast as it heads toward the bleachers for a home run to make the score 2-1.

"Way to go, Trayce," Tom yells loudly as he puts his arm around Katie.

Her reaction is far different from the usual exuberance and feistiness that are such a big part of Katie's day to day existence. This time she's barely responsive and mutters to her husband.

"Tommy, I'm having my first contraction. I don't want to go to the hospital right now, unless absolutely necessary. I have to see the end of this game," Katie says as she turns to Tom. "There, it's over and I feel OK. That couldn't have been any more than 30 to 40 seconds."

"Nonsense, I'll call and send a text to the paramedics in the first aid room and have them come to our seats right now," Tom quickly replies. "Let's have them check on your condition and determine if you should get to the hospital immediately. We don't want you to give birth right here at the ballpark with this huge crowd and all the chaos everywhere. I'm also going to call and text Dr. Leonard. Hopefully she'll be able to get to Mercy Hospital in plenty of time for the delivery."

Tom and Katie barely notice as Hendricks gets the next three batters out, leaving the score at 2-1 Cubs going into the top of the third. Tom's phone starts to ring and he becomes involved in a brief conversation, which Katie knows is about her situation.

"The paramedic said if it's just one short contraction, it's too early to think about going to the hospital. He also emphatically urged us to time them, in frequency and length, and call him when they're stronger and less than 10 minutes apart. So for now, we'll just try to enjoy the game," Tom explains.

"Easy to say, but now, all of a sudden, this colossal World Series match-up between the White Sox and Cubs, seems very secondary," Katie blurts out. "We've dreamed of seeing a game of such importance for much of our lives and now something far more important is about to happen."

"I certainly feel the same way!" Tom seconds what she says.

The Cubs get two more men on base with one out in the third. That brings up Rizzo again, who cracks a hard single up the middle, scoring Montero from second base to make it 3-1. Bryant follows with another hard hit, but it's a ground ball right at second baseman Sanchez, who quickly turns it into a double play.

Despite her situation and knowing she'll soon be going to the hospital for one of the most exciting events in her life, Katie is still thrilled that the Cubs have a 3-1 lead in this game of games, but with less fervor than would usually be the case.

Her enthusiasm wanes even more after the White Sox begin to peck away at Hendricks in the bottom of the third. Catcher Vlessen starts things off with a bunt single, surprising everyone in the ballpark as he lays down a perfect "small hit" along the third base line.

Sanchez goes after the first pitch and lines a shot past Rizzo down the right field line that takes a nasty ricochet away from right fielder Soler, back in the lineup despite having a sore ankle, once it hits the wall in the corner. By the time the ball is back in the infield, Vlessen crosses home plate and Sanchez is standing on third with a triple and the potential tying run.

"Oh my God!" Katie lashes out. "Why can't the Cubs hold a lead in their most important game in over a century?"

"Relax, sweetheart," Tom tells her. "The Cubs might still win this game. At this point my feeling is the big winner here is this great place where we are fortunate to live. And you and I are the biggest winners of all with our family about to expand!"

As Tom is talking, Eaton is delivering for the White Sox with a long fly ball out to center field which scores Sanchez to tie the score at 3-3. And it's only been three innings! This certainly figures to be a game with a lot of hits and runs scored.

But not in the fourth or fifth, Johnson and Hendricks each retire the side in order in both innings as the feeling of tension on Chicago's South side only thickens.

The sixth inning brings a new pitcher for each team. Petricka, the middle inning reliever who is inconsistent at times but often gets the job done, starts the sixth on an ominous note by walking Bryant.

Clean-up hitter Soler, the next batter, squares as if to bunt, but can only manage a weak pop-up behind catcher Vlessen. He quickly jumps up, throws down his mask and makes the catch for the first out.

Schwarber hits a long fly ball to right fielder Garcia, which backs him up to the wall for the second out. That's followed by a ground out to end the half-inning.

Strop comes in to take the mound for the Cubs in the bottom of the sixth. He gets the first two batters, then gives up a double to Eaton, but gets out of any further trouble with a strikeout.

Tom, meantime, receives a return call from Dr. Evelyn Leonard, Katie's OB-GYN. She wants to talk with her and also urges him to get Katie to the hospital very soon, before it's too congested and crowded to get away from the ballpark.

"But we're just going into the seventh inning. She hasn't had a second contraction yet and Mercy Hospital is only about two miles away along the Stevenson Expressway at 23rd," Tom explains, as he hands his phone to his wife. "Here, it's Dr. Leonard to talk with you."

"Yes, Dr. Leonard. Oh, I'm feeling pretty good and am indeed very excited," Katie tells her.

"Well, don't stay there too much longer. Just get to Mercy as soon as possible. I've called to alert the maternity floor you'll be coming there from the ballpark very soon," the doctor tells her. "I'll be leaving my office on Fullerton in a few minutes and should be there within a half hour, even with the terrible traffic."

Tom takes the phone from Katie and calls Jeff to let him know they're ready to depart for Mercy Hospital.

"Good, you don't want to take any chances. I'm already heading toward your seats to get the car keys and your parking lot ticket. I'll get there within a matter of minutes," Jeff quickly replies.

By this time the top of the seventh inning is almost over. Petricka returns from the dugout and strikes out the first two overanxious batters on 3-2 counts, bringing huge cheers from the largely pro-White Sox crowd But shortstop Russell jumps on the first pitch he sees and sends it far over the left field fence and beyond the White Sox bullpen to give the Cubs a 4-3 lead.

The city explodes into cheers with long-suffering fans of the North Siders ecstatic with joy. Would Russell become the hero of not just this night, but for eternity and have his name forever etched into Chicago history books?

"It's the greatest home run I've ever seen," Katie screams while she tightly hugs Tom and gives him a gigantic kiss as tears roll down her cheeks. "I couldn't be happier."

Suddenly she flinches and yells loudly, "A huge contraction. I'm having a huge contraction."

Tom quickly looks at the second hand on his watch, watches it go around once and then another 15 seconds around again. He calls the paramedic he's been in touch with at the ballpark to let him know about the 75-second contraction, but there's no answer.

He then sends a text as the half-inning ends and runs to get help from an usher who is on a walkie-talkie transmitter learning about some kind of emergency elsewhere in the ballpark.

"There's a big brawl going on under the left field stands between groups of White Sox and Cubs fans. Even with the added police presence here tonight, it's out of control and the paramedics are dealing with a bunch of injuries and getting people to Mercy and other local hospitals once more ambulances arrive," the usher hurriedly explains.

"It started with a battle for the Russell home ball between Cubs and Sox fans and quickly got out of control. A lot of the security people, Chicago police and paramedics are out there trying to calm everyone down.""

"Well, my wife is about to have a baby or maybe even twins," Tom tells him. "We've got to get help for her."

Just then Jeff comes running up and tells Tom about the melee going on several sections away in left field.

"Everyone involved is going crazy, arguing about who caught the ball and which team is going to win this historic game," Jeff explains.

"It's somewhat reminiscent of the major skirmish that involved numerous fans fighting like crazy on Waveland Avenue on September 12, 1998. They were hoping to grab Sammy Sosa's 60th home run ball that season, making him the fourth player in major league history after Babe Ruth, Roger Maris and Mark McGwire to reach that once seemingly impossible number. Barry Bonds, of course, surpassed that group later."

"Let's just get both of you out of here right now and not wait around for any paramedics. I'll drive your car. You and Katie can be in the back. Hopefully, you're not blocked in where you're parked," suggests Jeff.

"I told the parking lot guys we might have to make a quick emergency exit to get Katie to the hospital. They took one look at her and knew what I was talking about. We're also parked on the right field side of the park, so we don't have to go anywhere near that ruckus on our way out," replies Tom. "We need to see if there's a policeman who will walk us to the car. There should be plenty of them with all the security around this place."

The bottom of the seventh comes and goes quickly for the White Sox against another relief pitcher, right-hander Justin Grimm.

They get to the car, parked in a lot on Shields Avenue, without incident amid a gigantic number of other vehicles. Fans are swarming around U.S. Cellular Field from all over the city to be part of the post-game celebration for whichever team wins.

"Wow, this may be a nightmare getting to Mercy, even though it's such a short distance away. Once we start heading north, away from the park, it should ease at bit. Hopefully, there will be officers at the corners directing traffic who can help us get through," Tom says.

"Let me deal with the driving," Jeff hastily replies as he turns on the car radio to the ballgame on WLS-AM (890), the one-time famous Prairie Farmer station, then later a rock and roll powerhouse for decades. "I'll get us there."

At that moment, Katie feels another contraction starting, this time much stronger and sure to last longer. "Another contraction," she whimpers. "It really hurts and we just have to get to the hospital very quickly."

"We'll get you there honey. I promise," Tom says as he comforts her and puts a blanket around her. "Just keep breathing slowly and try to relax the best you can between the contractions."

He next calls Dr. Leonard, who has now arrived at the hospital, to let her know they're on their way and will hopefully be at Mercy within 15 minutes.

"Katie dear, Dr. Leonard is already at Mercy and says she'll be outside the emergency room entrance waiting for us," Tom excitedly says.

Jeff pulls the car out of the lot toward Pershing Road, even though it's further south and a bit out of the way. Traffic is slow but creeping along. They turn left onto Pershing and head toward Michigan Avenue.

As they drive, the voice of longtime radio announcer and one-time Sox pitcher Ed Farmer excitedly bellows out of the console. It's now the bottom of the 8th inning with the Sox frantically trying to tie the game or even go ahead.

As they get to Michigan Avenue and turn left to head toward the hospital, Farmer screams over the radio, "It's a triple for Avasail Garcia with one out here in the bottom of the eighth. Now we have two chances this inning to bring in the tying run with Ramirez now up. Come on, Alexei."

"Oh, shit," Katie weakly exclaims. "Please don't get this run in. Let the Cubs win."

Tom has a different notion. "You'd better get that run in, Alexei," he loudly hollers, almost blasting Katie's ear off.

The drama is short-lived when Farmer yells out, "There's a line drive into center field for a base hit. The White Sox have tied it 4-4. Ramirez gets the game tying hit off Hector Rondon."

Just then, Jeff pulls into the emergency room parking lot and tries to weave his way around the throng of cars. Tom spots Dr. Leonard and rolls down the window to yell to her. With all the commotion going on with ambulances arriving from the melee at the ballpark, she can't hear him and they can't get any closer to the door

Jeff says, "Why don't you and Katie get out here. I'll go park the car where I can and find you. I know it'll take a few minutes to get Katie checked in and upstairs to the maternity area."

"Great idea," responds Tom. "C'mon, sweetheart. Let's get out and find Dr. Leonard. You should be able to walk that far before we get a wheelchair or gurney for you."

"I'll try," answers Katie, "but it's getting more difficult to move around."

"Ok, I'll get out and find her. You wait here. Is that okay with you, Jeff?"

"Good idea. We'll be right here."

Tom jumps out of the car running as fast as he can to find Dr. Leonard. She finally spots him and begins moving toward him along with a nurse pushing a gurney for Katie.

"Thank goodness you spotted us. Katie is having more contractions and is getting totally upset about making it to the labor room in time," Tom explains to the doctor.

Right then, Katie makes a loud grunt. "I think my water just broke. Oh, where are Tom and Dr. Leonard? I need to get into the hospital right now!"

"Katie, I see them moving quickly toward us. They should be here in less than a minute. You'll be fine until then. Dr. Leonard will take over as soon as she sees you and you'll be in her wonderful care," Jeff says to reassure her.

Meantime, Farmer tells us on the radio that the Cubs have a man on first with one out and Rizzo up in the top of the ninth, facing Sox closer David Robertson.

Katie says, "Anthony, for me and whoever is about to be born, please get this run home!"

As she finishes her prayer for a big hit, the car door opens and in front of her are Tom, Dr. Leonard and a young man and woman, both nurses, with a gurney.

"Dr. Leonard, my water just broke!" she exclaims.

"You're doing great. Just relax and stay calm. We'll get you into the delivery room in just a couple of minutes. Let them put you on the gurney," the doctor replies.

As that's happening, Katie hears out of a different radio longtime Cubs play-by-play voice Pat Hughes describe a great catch on WSCR (670) by Cabrera on a long drive to left center by Rizzo, saving a run. Her body deflates as the nurses carefully slide her out of the car lift her onto the gurney. All she seems to notice are masses of people and police everywhere around her.

Next thing she sees is Tom leaning over and kissing her, then looking at his phone and saying, "Sox are batting in the bottom of the ninth. What a game!"

They rush Katie to the elevator to get her upstairs and prepped for the delivery. Meantime, Tom is told by Dr. Leonard to go to admitting and quickly fill out the necessary paperwork.

"No, I need him here with me for support and to watch our child being born," Katie cries out as she's being wheeled onto the elevator.

They pass Jeff in the hallway, who is heading to the maternity floor himself after parking the car, to anxiously sit in the waiting room. He's also got a phone in his hand following the game.

"Good luck, Katie. I just called your and Tom's parents to let them know this is the real game going on right now. They're all racing here to be with you and Tom," Jeff says.

"Don't worry. Tom will be with us very soon. I've already alerted admitting that he's on his way to get you registered quickly. It's going to take several minutes before you'll be ready to deliver," Dr. Leonard, a seemingly well-organized woman in her late 30s or early 40s, hurriedly says as the elevator doors open onto the maternity floor.

"Let's get you into a room, get you prepped and attach a monitor so we can follow what's happening with your baby," Dr. Leonard continues. "By the time we do that, Tom should be up here to help you with your breathing routine."

The nurses get Katie ready and attach the monitor.

"Oh, my goodness! I hear two heartbeats very clearly now. I don't know where the second one has been hiding, but you're definitely going to have twins. No doubt about it now," announces the doctor.

"Wow!" comes from a voice just entering the room. It's Tom, who's both flabbergasted and delighted with the news. "We might actually have both a Gabby and a Frank! Either that or we'll have to figure out names quickly if it's two girls or two boys."

Katie tries to laugh at her wonderful husband, but just then feels another contraction coming on. "I'm so happy you're here," she says to him as she tightly grabs onto his hand.

"Okay, Katie. Remember how to breathe." Tom says looking at his beautiful wife. "Short breaths out like you're panting. It's what they taught us to do in our birthing class. Right?"

Dr. Leonard is watching the monitor and says, "Okay, we're going to get you into the delivery room. Tom can wash up and put on a gown to be with you. Let's go!"

As Katie is wheeled a few doors down, with Tom by her side, they briefly are stopped by a room with the WOLF network broadcast of the game, now in the bottom of the 10th inning. They hear play-by-play sportscaster Joe Buck's description of a long fly ball by Abreu that's caught for the third out of the inning, sending it to the 11th and exchange a quick glance.

They get to the delivery room where everything is ready for her arrival.

"Katie, when I tell you, I need you to push and then to stop when I say 'stop'," Dr. Leonard explains. "Tom, I need you to keep her breathing regularly and make her feel relaxed, as much as she can be at this point. Before you know it, you'll be parents of healthy twins!"

"OK, Katie, push! And keep pushing."

After about 10 minutes of stopping and starting, Dr. Leonard sees a head begin to emerge. "Keeping pushing, Katie. Baby number one is almost here."

Just then, a loud cry is heard by everyone. "What a loud, healthy cry for your new daughter," says Dr. Leonard as she has Tom cut the umbilical cord. Then she lifts up the baby to show Katie her new daughter.

"Do you know what her name will be?" the doctor asks. "Yes," says Katie. "She's Gabrielle Minnie, after Gabby Hartnett and Minnie Minoso."

"What a great name! Now, just relax for a few minutes before your next contraction and we find out whether it's another girl or a boy," the doctor says. "Whichever it is, he or she certainly did a great job of hiding from all of us and our tests. By the way, Gabrielle weighs 5 pounds, 2 ounces and is 21 inches long. That's pretty large for a twin. She was probably covering up baby number 2 because of her size. Time of birth: 11:08 pm."

During this quiet time, Katie and Tom are each wondering what is happening in the game. He takes a peak at his phone to see the situation. The game is still tied, now in the 12th inning.

Another contraction brings a grimace to Katie's face as Tom continues to comfort her.

"It won't be long now until baby number 2 arrives. I can sense he or she is getting very anxious to join the world," Dr. Leonard softly says. "This is the latest in a pregnancy where I've ever found out there was going to be twins. It's very unusual."

Right then, another contraction hits Katie and she yells out loudly, "Just be born already. It hurts!"

Within a few more minutes, Dr. Leonard sees the baby's head appear. "It's time. Katie, give me a big push. That looks like it's all we need to meet the newest member of your family."

With that said, there's a loud squeal from Katie as the baby comes out with a long, loud cry.

"This time it's a boy! He's born at 11:12 pm and looks very healthy. Let's get him weighed and measured. Do you have a name for your son?" the doctor asks.

Tom answers, "Yes, he's Frank Ernie Buchanan, named after Hall of Famers Frank Thomas and Ernie Banks. What a wonderful night. Now we just have to see who won the seventh game."

The nurse has finished weighing and measuring their son and reports, "He's 5 pounds and 20 inches long."

"Congratulations to both of you. I know you wanted to hold off until after the game ends, but these two wanted to be here for that moment, too. I'm thrilled to have been a part of this incredible event," declares Dr. Leonard. "I understand there's a big group of your family and friends already here to meet Gabby and Frank. Katie, let's get you cleaned up and to your room where they can rotate briefly visiting you. They'll be able to come for a longer period tomorrow, but right now you need to rest and get some sleep."

Katie and Tom, both with tears running down their faces, nod to the doctor.

"Tom, while we finish here with Katie, why don't you go out to the waiting room and tell everyone the great news. Katie will be in Room 1034 in about half an hour with the babies," Dr. Leonard suggests.

"That's great! I can't wait to tell everyone about Gabby and Frank," Tom replies. "Our parents and friends will be thrilled and shocked about the twins. No one expected that to happen."

Upon entering the waiting room, Tom is surprised to see that the baseball match-up is still ongoing. It's now the 14th inning, the longest World Series game 7 in history, still tied 4-4. He still hopes the White Sox will win, but at this point is convinced both teams are winners to him.

"Well, I have great news! Katie and the babies are doing well and you'll get to meet Gabby and Frank very soon. You can each just spend a few moments with them tonight. Katie needs her rest. It's been a long night for her and all of us," Tom explains.

Jeff approaches Tom and says with tears in his eyes, "Thank you for letting me be a part of this wonderful happening. I'm glad I was able to be of some help and honored to get to know you and become friends." He then gives Tom a big hug and pulls a large envelope out of his pocket which he describes as a baseball starter kit for the babies. He also hands him a small bag which Tom opens and sees both a Cubs and White Sox baby-sized T-shirt in it.

"You and Katie can decide which twin gets which shirt," Jeff suggests.

Once everyone leaves Katie's room, both Katie and Tom quickly fall asleep with the World Series championship still in doubt. Right now, they know they are the biggest winners of all.

The game, meantime, progresses into the bottom of 15th inning when the White Sox put runners on first and third with one out and catcher Vlessen at bat.

Knowing he's a slow runner, Maddon has the infield play back in hopes of getting an inning-ending double play,

Just like the genius he has proven to be since first putting on a Cubs uniform, the manager is right on target. Vlessen bounces what appears to be a tailor-made double play ball to shortstop Russell. But he briefly bobbles it, giving Vlessen a chance, albeit slim, to beat the throw from second to first.

Rizzo does the splits and stretches his athletic body as far as he possibly can to catch second baseman Castro's throw before Vlessen's foot touches the bag. It's ever so close, just a microsecond either way as to whether he's safe or out, and if the World Series ends with the White Sox winning or continues into the 16th inning.

Either way, whatever the umpire's call, you know it's going to be reviewed via replay, regardless of which manager demands it Thousands of die-hard baseball fans feared something like this could eventually happen once the umpire's call no longer was the ultimate word and now it's become a reality. A video replay is about to decide the outcome of the most important baseball game of the year and perhaps ever in the City of Chicago.

We'll let them hash this out and you can decide who wins the 2016 Crosstown Chicago World Series. The real winners are the people of Chicago, whether baseball fans or not, who have been able to enjoy this classic series of games.

To sum it all up, it was legendary sports writer Red Smith of the *New York Herald Tribune* who penned these famous words in 1951, after Bobby Thomson's famous walk off home run gave the then New York Giants the National League pennant. He said: "Now it is done. Now the story ends. And there is no way to tell it. The art of fiction is dead. Reality has strangled invention. Only the utterly impossible, the inexpressibly fantastic, can ever be plausible again." (77)

Congratulations to both teams!

ABOUT THE AUTHOR

Steve Corman is an eight-time Emmy-award winning television and radio news and sports producer / writer.

He has nearly 50 years of experience and has worked at WMAQ-TV (NBC-Chicago), KNSD-TV (NBC—San Diego) and WIND Radio (Group W—Chicago) in a variety of producing, writing and management positions.

Steve also has taught courses in writing and television production at several different colleges and universities in both the Chicago and San Diego areas.

In addition, he is the author of "Danny's Decades," a semi-biographical novel about a young boy who has visions of becoming a journalist. Steve and his wife, Sheila, now reside in the San Francisco Bay Area, in Alameda.

ACKNOWLEDGMENTS

A venture of this magnitude needs plenty of help and support to make it work and be successful.

Heading this impressive list is none other than "Sweet Little" Sheila Corman, my bride of over 48 years. She's been a vital part of my life and her support in this effort has been never-ending, as a researcher-editor and incorporating her many wonderful skills as a librarian, wordsmith and into giving this book the magic touch it needs.

Our adult children, Lisa, an attorney, and Neil, a photographer and computer software specialist, also greatly contributed. Even our granddaughter, Hannah, and son-in-law, Paul, himself an award winning writer, have been instrumental.

Going back in time, Dr. John Munski, my high school journalism teacher and advisor to the school paper, was a huge influence about always reporting the truth. He also was the first "non-medical doctor" I ever knew. That's when I learned what being a Ph.D. was all about.

At the University of Denver, J. Russell Heitman headed the journalism department after a long-time career as a community newspaper editor. He was the force behind my obsession with the "A-B-Cs" of accuracy, brevity and clarity in putting stories together, whether for broadcast or print.

I also was fortunate to work with a brilliant writer on our school paper, the *Denver Clarion.* The late Bella Stumbo eventually became a Pulitzer Prize winner at the *Los Angeles Times* and later wrote several books.

In the working world, Bill Berg, Dave Baum and Charles Cleveland, longtime friends and colleagues at WIND radio (Group W-Chicago), were forever offering advice and providing great encouragement and praise along with it.

At WMAQ-TV (NBC-Chicago), the list of those who greatly influenced me over nearly two decades is endless. It includes fellow producer-writers Art Cerf, Meg Moritz, Patricia Dean, Doug Manning, Don Moseley, Marjorie Fox, Ann Serafin and Scott Hooker; sports producers Bill Gutman, Jeff Davis and Aldo Perri; anchor-reporters Carol Marin, Jim Ruddle, Ron Magers, Jorie Lueloff, Mike Leiderman, Barry Bernson, Al Lerner, Rich Samuels and Dick Kay.

Once I followed Horace Greeley's advice to go West and wound up as Executive Producer and Managing Editor at KNSD-TV (NBC-San Diego), there also are many who played a significant role in my work. They start with News Director Irv Kass, anchor-reporters Marty Levin, Gene Cubbison, Ame Koeppel, Jack Gates, Doug Curlee, Kim Devore, Richard Harrison and sports anchor Jim Stone.

During my college teaching days, professors, instructors and students alike captivated me and I in turn will never forget them. They include professors Evan Wirig, Al Parker, Ed Planer, Ed Morris, Jim Disch, Sara Livingston, Norma Green, Carolyn Hulse, Jim Sulski and Rose Economou.

Former students who have moved on to excel at broadcast facilities around the nation are: Jamie Innis Justice, Shelby Croft, Lisa Manna Hartlund, Robert Stevenson, Jan Thompson Kraig and Mike Johnson, just to name a few.

I'm very appreciative to everyone mentioned here, as well as a enormous array of others.

Steve Corman

FOOTNOTES & REFERENCES

Chapter 1

1. "1906 World Series," www.Wikipedia. org.
2. "Year by Year Results," www.Seattle.Mariners.mlb.com.
3. "1906 World Series," WhiteSoxInteractive.com.

Chapter 2

4. "Historic Marker: West Side/ Grounds." www.historyillinois.com.
5. 1906 World Series attendance, www.baseballreference.com.
6. Lindberg, Richard C., *The White Sox Encyclopedia.* Philadelphia: Temple University Press, 1997. Page 428.
7. Ibid, Page 428.
8. "Mordecai Brown," sabr.org/bioproj/.
9. Op.cit. (WSE). Page 429.
10. Op.cit. (WSE). Page 212.
11. "Johnny Kling," sabr.org/bioproj./.

Chapter 3

12. "List of Cubs Seasons," www.Wikipedia.org.
13. "List of White Sox Seasons," www.Wikipedia.org.
14. "Statement of Commissioner Landis, August 4, 1921," Law2.umkc.edu.
15. "1945 World Series," www.Wikipedia.org.
16. "Curse of the Billy Goat," www.Wikipedia.org.
17. "Emil Verban," www.Wikipedia.org
18. "Timeline: Cubs Ownership," www.Chicago.Cubs.mlb.com.
19. "Cubs Fire Rick Renteria," www.mlbtraderumors.com, October 31, 2014.
20. "Jon Lester, Cubs Agree to a 6-year deal," www.usatoday.com, December 10, 2014.
21. Ibid, www.mlbtraderumors.com.

Chapter 4

22. "Wrigley Field Construction," www.ooyuz.com, April 2, 2015.
23. "New-look Cubs Display Familiar Shortcomings," www.chicagotribune.com, April 5, 2015.

24. "Cubs Firmly Believe They Are Better Than Record," www.chicagotribune.com, April 10. 2015.

25. "All-Star Game Berth Likely for Cubs Phenom," www.chicagotribune.com, Ma7, 27, 2015.

26. "Phillies Pitcher Cole Hamels No-Hits Cubs," www.si.com, July 25, 2015.

27. "Rizzo Homers in 4th Straight Game," www.ap.org, August 1, 2015.

28. "Rapid Reaction: Tigers 15, Cubs 8," www.espn.go.com, August 1, 2015.

29. "Everyone Saw Kris Bryant's Monster Home Run," www.espn.go.com, September 6, 2015.

30. "Starlin Castro's 2 Homers, 6 RBIs," scores.espn.go.com, September 18, 2015.

31. "Bryant and John Mallee," *Sarasota Herald Tribune,* September 19, 2015.

32. "Cubs Rewarding Maddon's Optimism," www.mlb.com, September 7, 2015.

33. "Joe Maddon Remembers First Day with Cubs," www.cubs.mlb.com, October 12, 2015.

34. "With Extra Day of Rest before Game 2, Jake Arrieta Should Be Strong," *Chicago Tribune*, October 17, 2015.

35. "Cubs Really Up Against Wall After Losing Third Straight to Mets in NCLS," www.chicagotribune.com, October 21, 2015.

36. "NCLS Was a Major Downer, But Things Are Still Looking Up for the Cubs," www.chicagotribune.com, October 22, 2015.

37. "After Ugly Ending Fades, Cubs' Beautiful Season Will be Recalled Warmly," www.chicagotribune.com, October 22, 2015.

38. "White Sox Slugger Abreu Joins Pujols," www.chicagotribune.com, October 2, 2015.

39. "White Sox Check Out Early…" www.chicagosuntimes.com, April 29, 2015.

40. Ibid.

41. "Stirring the Drink," www.beachwoodreporter.com, May 11, 2015.

42. "The Amazing Story of Carlos Rodon," www.baseballnews.com, December 20, 2013.

43. "Sale Becomes 3rd Player in MLB History," www.bleacherreport.com, June 19, 2015.

44. "Sale Named AL Player of Month for June," www.wgntv.com, July 2, 2015.

45. "Sale's 8th 10-Strikeout Game Ties Record," www.mlb.com, August 16, 2015.

46. "Chris Sale Strikes Out 15 to End Cubs' Streak," www.mlb.com, August 16, 2015.

47. "Olt lst Player to Home for Cubs, Sox in Same Year, www.chicago.suntimes.com, , September 16, 2015.

48. "Abreu Joins Exclusive HP, RBI Club," www.mlb.com, October 1, 2015.

49. Ibid.

50. "Sale Sets Single-Season K-Mark," www.mlb.com, October 3, 2015.

51. "Hahn: Ventura Returning in 2016," www.chicago.sintimes.com, October 2, 2015.

52. "Ventura Talks About Second Half," www.wgnradio.com, July 9, 2015.

Chapter 6

53. "Yearly League Leaders in Sacrifice Bunts," www.baseball-reference.com.

54. "In a First, World Series Game Suspended," www.mlb.com, October 28, 2008.

55. "10 Rainiest Weather Days in Chicago**,"**
www.Chicago-il.knoji.com.

Chapter 8

56. "South Side Park," www.Wikipedia.com.

57. "Ed Reulbach," www.sabr.org/bioproj/person.

58. Op.cit. (WSE), pages 199-200.

Chapter 9

59. "Lester Diagnosed with Form of Lymphoma,"
www.sports.espn.go.com, September 3, 2006.

60. "Inside USD," www.sandiego.edu. June 4,
2013.

61. "New Arizona Coach Tips Cap to Bryant,"
www.chicagotribune.com, June 6, 2015.

Chapter 10

62. "Big Ed Walsh," www.sabr.org.

63. Op. Cit. (WSE), pp. 143-144.

64. "Jack Pfiester," www.sabr.org.

Chapter 12

65. Op.cit (WSE), pages 141-142.

66. "Harry Steinfeldt," www.sabr.org.

Chapter 14

67. "List of MLB Doubles Records," www.Wikipedia.com.

68. "Frank Isbell," www.sabr.org.

69. "Jimmy Sheckard," www.sabr.org.

Chapter 16

70. "World Series Gate Receipts," www.baseball-almanac.com.

71. "SF Giants Get Record Bonuses," www.bizjournals.com, November 14, 2015.

72. Op. cit. (WSE), pages 238-239.

73. "Frank Schulte," www.sabr.org.

Chapter 17

74. "Carlos Rodon Ready for City Series, Wrigley," www.chicagotribune.com, July 9, 2015

Chapter 20

75. "TV Ad Pricing Chart," www.adage.com, September 24, 3015.

76. "Super Bowl 49 Ad Chart," www.adage.com, January 30, 2015.

77. "Thomson Authored Unlikely Ending," Red Smith, www.espn.go.com, October 4, 1951, Excerpt from "Red Smith on Baseball".

www.ingramcontent.com/pod-product-compliance
Lightning Source LLC
Chambersburg PA
CBHW070457030726
47503CB00004B/1081